JUNGLE OF ECLIPSES

BY NEVELIOUS JORDAN

S ight heightened Earth's metaphysical consciousness long before the planet was overpopulated. With it, the elements saw their reflection and the eventual creation of man. They soon witnessed the barbarism and greed that humans are capable of, watching themselves be polluted and commodified.

To preserve their sanctity, they split their consciousnesses. Half created the Celortus, beings that allowed them to speak and feel emotions. The other half created their protectors, who draw their might from elemental empowerment.

These are the graced children. They are the Elehominum.

The Library's hidden entrance, 2017

CHAPTER I

The Elehominum's expedition through the orange portal was preceded by twirls of colors. Deep purples and vibrant pinks intermeshed at obtuse angles, creating shimmering twinkles. Coasting along milky foam ripples, they arrived at a white stone site situated on a ground of hardened salt. Stretching to a star-filled sky, forty-foot-high monoliths overlooked a dinosaur bone pileup. Bright flashes peeked out of the hollowed sockets of a broken skull that sat at the top.

Miniature hourglasses surrounded the primitive remains. Some were three-quarters full, others completely depleted.

"These all can't be counting down to Earth's apocalypse. Wish we had a clue to tell us what the heck they're for," whispered Julien.

Peering about their surroundings, the graced children saw what elevated the rock-threaded pillars: revolving black globes. Chunks of pebbles floated by them, exuding an orange mist around what appeared to be the top cap and rungs of a carbon ladder halfway stuck in the ground.

"Alright, everybody," Julien started. "Same strategy:

stay close and be alert. We can't afford anyone else getting hurt."

Teal-glowing glyphs lit the surface as they drew nearer. Planets arose from the markers, aligning themselves in order of largest to smallest. Jupiter, Saturn, and Uranus rotated at a snail's pace. Neptune bounced wildly, leaking hydrogen sprinkles. The other five jiggled in a sepia radiance.

Protective of the still-unconscious girl in his arms, Noah was careful not to let Piper's arms or legs dangle. He walked slowly, untrusting of the peculiar environment.

Blair looked to the peak of the nearest monolith, her green eyes sparking with electricity as she inched forth. "I betcha that rat bastard Navi'el is hidin' behind one of these."

"Hey, Bee, I don't think you should try climbing. It might be best to just…"

The monolith's globe rumbled, interrupting Julien's suggestion. Its prime meridian sprayed an odorless, clear liquid that shaped itself into a rectangular prism. A rainy forestland rich with cotton fields was visualized. Crows with human faces and hairless sheep were most notable of the introductory images.

Stored memories of Navi'el serving thick cutlets of a dark meat to minotaurs were then simulcasted. They ate merrily until their lips swelled and their legs went limp. Clustering them together, he proceeded to scalp each. Hands bound to their buttocks, the bull-man hybrid victims were then made to watch him burn their crops. Gassy letters materialized, naming the habitat Valleys of Peace and confirming its destruction date of December 13, 2014.

"He's a liar and a cheat. That don't impress me none. If they knew what was up, they would've trampled him," commented Blair.

"I'm not so sure," Noah admitted, nodding at the great henge to his left. "Check this out."

The globe erecting it emitted a mirrorlike pentagon that reflected a levitating, majestic court in disrepair. Enormous eggs, cracked and oozing yolk, looped its dented rear. Dynamite sticks had leveled the citadel. Smashed gables sank to a bottomless pit of stardust.

Resting upon a cloud, armies of winged tarantulas worked to repair the castle's crumbling gothic architecture. The spiders spewed a slushy fluid that stabilized the setting. Ensuing chaos at the drawbridge rendered their restoration meaningless.

Swinging redwood-spiked clubs, Navi'el battled a scorpion the size of a cargo truck. He dodged its sweeping tail, the swipes intended for him obliterating the castle's foundation. Adjoining his weapons and leaping, the lone despoiler impaled the gigantic arachnid's underbelly. He sliced her ovary open, and withdrew a bloodied sapphire diadem.

The flying tarantulas swarmed their matriarch's killer but did not attack. They instead formed a line, obediently lowering themselves to his feet. He snapped the jeweled headband, erasing them and their palace. The memory fizzled and those gassy letters reappeared, identifying the queendom as the Venusian Empire of Arachnida and its destruction date of September 3, 1943. Cobwebs entangled the vowels and numbers.

"Now we know where Emily got her sashes," inferred Blair. "She chatted all that royal rubbish, even though the slut was lovin' a thief. I'd pay a lot of money to hear her excuses. Too bad she ain't here to see us stomp a mudhole in Navi'el's ass."

"Speak of the devil," Julien said, watching a burst of blue rays, dripping rainwater, streak toward the furthest monolith's mouth.

"Emily's grace. Must've just left her body," suggested Noah. "But Father Nigel taught me and Piper that the process usually takes hours."

The purged essence drove into a smile-shaped nook, temporarily illuminating it in a violet radiance.

"Something tells me it's headin' where Navi'el's gone," Blair reputed.

"Only one way to be sure," agreed Julien, prepared to lead the chase.

Rattling, half of the dinosaur bones assembled into a skeletal Tyrannosaurus. Silver flames engulfed its ribcage. Sifting through the dusty jumble, it armed itself with the tail of a Velociraptor, and chose a Triceratops' head for a shield. Lurching, it bellowed a husky roar.

"Crap, should've known it wouldn't be *this* easy," Noah grumbled.

"Who cares?" remarked Blair, cracking her knuckles. "I'm gonna send ol' bonehead straight to Jurassic Park."

The prehistoric carnivore ran around them with dizzying speed. "I am the guardian of the gates. Safe passage is granted to those who can solve the last visitor's riddle."

"Nah, we're done with riddles; we'd rather be throwin' hands," Blair declined.

"We should be saving our energy," overruled Julien.

"And we have questions that need answering."

Cracking the tail like a whip, the gatekeeper hunched over them. "I do not make bargains. You may ask one."

"What is this place?" Julien inquired.

"The Omnipotent Continent. Travelers who have discovered the pathway in can revisit the historical destruction of near and far lands, and plunge from world to world," explained the gatekeeper.

"So, the stones are gates," Noah assumed.

"Indeed, child," corroborated the gatekeeper, its stale breath blowing them to the edge of the most distant block. "You have exhausted your queries. Solve the riddle or fall to my blazes."

Catching his balance, Julien raised his hands in submission. "Okay, we'll play by your rules. Tell us the riddle."

A ticking pendulum clock appeared within the gatekeeper's inflamed midsection. Growing eight feet taller, it sprouted wings in the form of two feathered tongues on its back.

"When I am new, I cannot be seen at all, yet I bloom with each nightfall. And as I loom over the wall, listen and you will hear the lone wolf's call. What am I?"

"Flowers bloom. Our Kindred Spirits are wolves. Gotta be Nightjar Kush," answered Blair, referencing the Atlantean plant that had stabilized Piper.

The clock blurred, its minute hand spiraling faster.

"But Nightjar Kush has nothing to do with a wall; it grew from the ground in a cave, remember," Noah reminded. "My guess is a bat. They're sleep during the day and fly in the nighttime. Sometimes, the buggers hang on walls and wolves bark at them."

The clock spun faster, still.

"Ugh, wrong again. Fightin' is gonna be the only option if we don't hurry," huffed Blair.

"Give me a sec to think. I'll come up with something," Noah swore.

"Think harder, dammit," ordered Blair.

Ignoring his bickering classmates, Julien mentally replicated the riddle's specifics. He recalled an astronomy article he read in last month's edition of *Teen Scientist Today*. The author, a 14-year-old Californian, had perfectly described ecliptic longitude and cited examples.

"Got it. The answer is the moon," he yelled.

The gatekeeper collapsed into a stack of disconnected parts, its timer burning to shiny ashes. Writhing, the feathered tongues withered to a mushy soup. The broth shriveled and became an additional glyph.

"Came through in the clutch like ya always do," said Blair, playfully nudging Julien.

"Bloody brilliant, pal. Kept your wits while me and Sparky were losing ours," Noah commended.

Julien's cheeks warmed. "Was pretty obvious, guys. During a new moon phase, the moon is between the Earth and sun. The entire illuminated portion of the moon is on its backside, which is the half that we can't see. When there's a full moon, the Earth, moon, and sun are in approximate alignment, just like the new moon, but the moon is on the opposite side of the Earth. The sunlit part of the moon is facing us then, which means it's visible. The last part is simple: wolves howl at the moon."

"And here he goes, blabbin' about science. We're gonna need flashcards and erasable ink for when he does this," joked Blair.

"Be thankful I'm a nerd. We almost got our butts cooked," Julien noted.

"Aye, glad we weren't the guests of honor at the big weenie roast," disclosed Noah. "But we've still gotta cross over to the other side. I don't see any doorway, unless…"

"Unless what?" Blair bit.

"Emily's grace passed without trouble. Magical spells can easily disguise stuff. If these monoliths are actually portals themselves, we may be able to do the same," hypothesized Noah.

"No harm in trying," said Julien, curiously patting the monolith's edges.

The globe that upheld the stony formation divided into two halves. A rift tore at its midpoint, and they were sucked into a vacuum of darkness. The orange portal that facilitated their initial entrance hiccupped. Encased in ruby-red magma, a gem exuding steam drifted and entered the rift.

Cold air and screeching train wheels welcomed the Elehominum back to the mundane world. A navy-blue tinge filtered the night. They had emerged under a stone bridge, a strip of convenience stores and fast-food restaurants behind them. McDonald's orders could be heard in the distance, honking car horns drowning out meal specifications. Raindrops kissed them. The moisture caused the melanin of Julien's face to shine like a black diamond.

To their right was a luxury television store, its door wide open. Every piece of merchandise in the window was set to a static channel except the widest: a 55-inch Samsung. A greasy-haired journalist occupied the screen, reporting on a sudden string of blackouts plaguing the northeast of England.

"I have received word that much of Sunderland and Newcastle upon Tyne are without power, and are experiencing extreme floods. The Prime Minister is likely to issue a stay-at-home order that, if violated, is punishable by imprisonment. An unnamed militia has been making the rounds to evacuate citizens," he broadcasted.

"This has Navi'el's name written all over it," Blair concluded. "Wherever he is, we've gotta get there and stop him. Wonder where we're at, though."

Kneeling before a patch of grass, Julien picked up a damp newspaper. "The Northern Echo. Face-painted woman steals eggs from Greggs and is arrested. Turn to page seven for the full story."

"That's the Railway Viaduct, recognize it from me mam's old stamp collection," said Noah, eyeing the bridge's arches. "And that newspaper is printed locally, if I remember correctly. We've gotta be in Durham."

"Great, how far are we from Newcastle?" Julien questioned. "If we make it to our school, we can regroup and maybe talk to the Celortus. They'll have an idea of what we should do."

"Train will get us there in a tick; it's literally the next stop," informed Noah.

They set their sights on the now-empty platform a yard away. Upon reaching the tracks, Julien and Blair checked for traps, overturning flattened cardboard boxes. Both searched the rail fastening system, certain they would find signs of Navi'el's foot soldiers, but saw none.

Convinced of the area's security, they trod onto a bed of rocks and told Noah to do the same, but he was preoccupied with the tiny body squirming against his dirty polo.

Piper yawned and awoke. "Did we win?"

"You're alive, thank the gods," Noah cheered, hugging her tightly.

"And you're squeezing my liver," coughed Piper.

Noah angled her onto her own two feet. "Huh? Oh, yeah. Sorry about that. Happy yi survived, though, man. Things weren't looking good."

"Feelin' brand new," Piper declared, doing a jumping jack.

"Nothin' can keep a real one down," attested Blair.

"I think I speak for everyone when I say there's strength in numbers, and with you on the mend, we are a lot stronger," Julien said, smiling.

Piper grabbed Noah's hand and skipped ahead, plopping beside Blair. "Gan take more than some grubby little dart to get rid of me. Geordies are built to last. Reet, Noah?"

"Wey aye, pet," replied the pale boy, flexing his pitiful bicep.

"The train will probably be coming in a few. Let's get a move on," Julien instructed.

Crossing the tracks, they climbed up the platform's ledge. The group bunched together on their walk along its gray, lined pattern, the closeness generating warmth that fought the evening's chills. It was not until Piper stopped that they were separated.

"Wait. Where's Salvador and Ava?" she asked, frantically looking around.

"They, um, won't be joining us," confirmed Julien.

"Oh," Piper said.

"Was Ava's idea to use that Nightjar Kush to save yi. I made Salvador promise that he'd be your protector when we left to fight Emily," recounted Noah, resting his hand on her shoulder.

Piper's head drooped and she fidgeted with the buttons of her mangy dress. "I would have liked to thank them for fighting with us. I could've given Salvador his last rites, but I didn't even get to say goodbye."

"It might not make ya feel any better but at least they weren't killed in battle," Blair said. "They chose not to come, and I can totally understand why. Those weird injections Dr. Jung was givin' 'em only work if they're taken daily; without 'em, they woulda aged forward and died. Ava and Salvador suffered enough abuse without havin' their youth sapped."

"I'm sick of me friends dying so often," mourned Piper, sinking onto an iron bench.

Noah bent and hugged her. Piper wrapped her arms around his neck and shed a silent tear. Blair threw her face in her hands, uncertain of what she could say to ease the girl's sorrow. Julien searched for the words of an uplifting speech, but incoming footsteps distracted him.

"Gimme wut's in da wallet, 'less man wants ta get cut!"

A tall, hooded man wearing a brown Patagonia coat intended to rob them. He aimed a butterfly knife at Julien's chest, but it was Blair who retaliated by dropping the mugger with a kick to his liver. She caught his airborne blade without blinking, and stood over him.

"I'm not losing anybody else," Piper screamed, running at the downed criminal.

Noah scooped her up by the waist, ignoring her demands to be let go.

"Relax. That knobhead could have something more than a knife on him," he argued, restraining her flailing appendages.

Noah's reasoning guided Julien's next actions. He stepped on the ruffian's ashy fingers and spoke directly to Blair.

"If this dude's not human, airhole him."

Ready to slit his throat, Blair detached the furry hood but did nothing more than squint.

"Paul, is that you?" she asked, removing his Jamaican bandana.

The mugger wheezed and breathed heavily. "Gyal, I told you wut mi name is now; it's Southside P, innit?"

"Is this dude a friend of yours?" questioned Julien, easing off his fingers.

"He's my ex," Blair said.

Shocked, Noah and Piper stopped their tussling.

Southside P hustled to a stand, his rhinestone earrings gleaming under the platform's lamplights. He was a shade lighter than Julien, and had the word "Brixton" tattooed above his left eyebrow. A neatly trimmed goatee boxed his mouth, but razor bumps blemished his jawlines.

"Guessin' dis dat Uncle Tom from dat posh school you got into. Shoulda kept doin' drills wif me instead ov hangin' wif a bumbaclot wannabe white boy. And wut's dat dey got him wearin'? Man's dressed like a janitor, tryna fit in wif white people."

Southside P's tactless discrimination reminded Julien of the trauma that came with that Noyeur Atlantis prison jumpsuit. "Excuse me? You can't imagine what I've been through. Who are you to judge my blackness?"

"Listen to di way you talk, bruv, it's all prim and proppa," Southside P criticized, dusting off his multi-zippered jeans. "Prolly never been in a fight or nuffin'. Spare me di tough talk; I don't believe it."

"Oh, you should believe it, because I wouldn't mind being in one right now," challenged Julien.

Blair shuffled between them, shoving her former boyfriend. "Na, this ain't happenin'. He don't got no beef with nobody. What're ya even doin' here?"

"Harder to jack people in London cuz da feds lookin' for me. Figured I'd slide to Durham and hit a couple ov licks. Man's gotta eat, ya get me," Southside P confessed, shrugging.

"Haven't got an ounce of shame, either. You'll never change. Ya only give a damn about yaself," rebuked Blair.

"Nuh, not true. I'll let you keep di knife, babes. Gunna need some protection when yer ridin' di train dis late, and it ain't comin' from dat goofy schoolboy," Southside P laughed, readjusting his hood as he descended a nearby staircase.

Julien glared at him, hoping he would trip on the untied laces of those Air Jordan 11 tennis shoes and shatter his chin.

"He wasn't very nice. His mam must not have

taught him manners," said Piper.

"Don't let him get to yi, mate. He's not worth the effort," Noah added.

Julien's attention diverted to the passenger information display. A schedule of departure times and locations scrolled across the monitor in red. The train to Newcastle would be arriving next. Swishing sounds and clanking metal signaled its speeding approach.

"He ain't on piss, anyhow," ridiculed Blair, pinning her hair up with the knife. "Chats like he's a hardcore goon, but he's too timid to pull a trigger. Anytime we did a drill, I was the shooter. Doped up on cancer meds, and he had me doin' drive-bys."

Julien scoffed, kicking the bandana onto the train tracks. "True, we've got more important stuff to be worried about than some hoodrat. Hopefully, everyone feels the same. Don't need any old flings distracting us."

"What's that supposed to mean?" Blair questioned.

"Nothing. Nothing at all," fibbed Julien.

CHAPTER II

A Virgin Super Voyager train raced into view. The curvy red and yellow lines painted onto its gray carts were slick with rainfall. Creeping to a halt, the steel vehicle's doors opened and a surplus of passengers outpoured. The majority were young and wearing 90s grunge band t-shirts, but there were also older people who held Bibles and spoke of God's love. The two groups seemed unlikely to have much in common yet they did; each remarked how horribly the Elehominum smelled as they departed.

"St. Michael's has an accommodation with showers, hun. Bishops wouldn't dare neglect a sweet child," a toothless woman said in passing.

Julien ignored her, directing their way aboard an empty cart. He led them to a bay of four blue denim seats. Blair plucked and crumpled the stiff tickets that reserved the space, and sat beside him.

"Ungrateful lot," griped Noah, sitting across from Julien. "Do they think we can save the world *and* change our underwear often?"

Piper sat next to him. "We shouldn't be talking about how we're saving the world. Father Nigel wouldn't want us telling."

"But isn't it obvious we ain't normal kids? We fought a giant crocodile in public, for Christ's sake. Somebody had to have seen that happen," Blair adduced.

"Yi forget most of Cumberchester Heights is the elderly and mentally disabled. Who's gan take their calls seriously," countered Noah.

Blair nudged Julien. "Somebody's gone mute. Ya alright?"

"I'm sleepy," he lied.

A robotic female voice announced Newcastle City Center as the next stop. The train took off. Fog shrouded treetops and telephone poles. Thunder clamored harshly outside, a theme for their homecoming.

"So, what's our backup plan if we can't call our Kindred Spirits," Piper asked.

"Maybe the Scarlet Gospels has a spell for instant kills. I've only just gotten to the section on fatal incantations," considered Noah, referencing the scroll that governed his grace. "I'll have a skim when we're at school."

"I dunno if goin' there's a smart decision. Navi'el might be plannin' an ambush if he thinks that's someplace we'd feel safe," Blair stated.

Julien stared out the window, his fingertips rapping absentmindedly on the glass.

"Yo," barked Blair. "Everyone is tired. Piper was almost killed, but her head's in the game. Let that sink in: she's 11-years-old and ain't askin' for a pacifier or a pillow. What the hell is your problem?"

Turning in his seat, Julien narrowed his eyes at her.

"My problem? Alright, I'll tell you. I'd like to know why you kept that thug's knife."

Blair's jaw dropped. "Oh, my days, bruv. This has gotta be a joke. You're the one that said we should be conservin' our energy. His knife could come in handy if we link with any of our opps."

"He's jealous," Noah smirked.

"What do I care," mumbled Julien, crossing his arms. "Blair can go marry Southstar Pea-brain or whatever that fake gangster calls himself."

"Don't be mean. I'm sure she doesn't want to," Piper mediated.

Blair scooted to the far edge of her seat. "Man's bein' immature and judgmental. Never would have expected it, not in a million years. I shoulda recognized the warning signs when you were arguin' with Salvador about his religion."

Pushing a refreshment carriage, a dumpy woman with mole-abundant cheeks approached them. The red blazer and blouse combination she sported was flawlessly ironed, and featured a name pin that labeled her as "Theresa H."

"Anything off the trolley, dears?"

Julien paid no attention to the stacks of potato chips, candy bars, and juices. He instead chose to side-eye Blair, who busied herself with spinning a Sprite bottle.

"Miss, times are really tough at our orphanage," fabricated Noah, pointing to the underarm stains of his polo. "We're very hungry, but have no money. It's been days since we last ate."

Their melded stench caused Theresa's heavy-lidded eyes to water. She covered her mouth with the cream linen handkerchief tied around her fat neck.

"Terribly sorry to hear. We aren't usually allowed to give free food, but I'll make a small exception."

"Oh, bless you, miss. You're a godsend," Noah cunningly praised, grabbing an armful of sugar-packed treats.

Theresa scoffed at his greed, driving the trolley onward before he could take more. She moved into the following cart, muttering about deodorant.

"Yi weren't honest; the Atlanteans fed us and we aren't orphans," frowned Piper.

Spreading the snacks among their seat trays, Noah tossed her a bag of salt and vinegar Walkers. "But that was ages ago. I kna yee stomach's rumbling, like."

"A lil' white lie ain't bad," Blair justified, unwrapping a watermelon Blow Pop. "They'll restock, and it ain't as if we're gettin' paid to risk our lives. We deserve a couple perks."

"Game the system. Did your ex teach you that?" quipped Julien.

Blair gave him the death stare. Her fists balled and she swallowed hard.

Sensing the tension, Noah cleared his throat. "Who gets the first crack at Navi'el? We could draw straws, or just knock that pansy back and forth like a pinball machine."

"Can't think of anybody I'd rather give a good whop," Piper confessed.

"Oh, but I can, and I will if he keeps actin' stupid," murmured Blair, crunching a piece of her lollipop.

Julien disregarded the veiled threat. "We aren't playing the lottery. I'm giving whoever is closest to him permission to punch his fricking lights out."

"Hope it's me. He'll be eating a knuckle sandwich," Piper said, chomping five chips at once.

"I would torture him and livestream it on the deep web," fantasized Noah. "Do something diabolical, like tape his eyes open and keep taking his picture."

After passing a towering pine-green bridge and a still river, the train's wheels loudly scraped the tracks. It swayed violently through a tunnel and crashed into a wall. Snacks and untagged luggage flew in every direction.

Piper held onto the buckle of her seatbelt. Noah tumbled toward the bathroom, narrowly avoiding a head-on collision with the door's bottom hinge. A weighted furry blanket had slid in front of the appliance, blocking its loose screws. Blair was thrown rightward, but Julien grabbed her wrist with one hand and an arm rest with his other.

"I'm ganna demand insurance," Noah complained, catching a can of Pepsi Max.

Jockeying herself to a stand, Blair yanked herself from Julien and hurried to press the emergency exit button. The train's doors creaked open.

"Shouldn't we check to see if anyone is hurt?" questioned Piper.

"Nuh uh," Julien rejected. "It's not a coincidence we crashed. Someone planned this. We're not giving them the opportunity to surprise us."

Noah guzzled the soda and tossed it aside. "Does have all the signs of a setup. The ride we needed just so happened to be coming not long after we got to the platform, and nobody asked if we had tickets. Quite obvious, aye?"

They exited one by one. Smoke billowed throughout

the vicinity. Glass splinters were scattered along the ground, bloody and uneven. The train's front half now resembled an accordion. Miraculously, an escape hatch unlocked and out crawled the conductor. His forehead was gashed down the middle and his upper lip had been completely severed. Lost teeth were wedged between the creases of his vest.

"It ran up...m-my leg," he stuttered, falling at Blair's feet. "Lost c-c-control when my chest was bitten."

"Stay here. We're going to find you a doctor," promised Julien.

Propping himself against a guardrail, the conductor rattled their eardrums with a jangling scream. A lab rat chewed through his left nipple, eating a three-course meal of polyester fabric, ingrown hairs, and mangled skin.

"That's a doomsday mouse from the prison," Julien discerned, recognizing its blistered humpback.

"Watch out," hollered Noah.

Scurrying off the train's dismantled side skirt, a second doomsday mouse dived at Julien's collar. Acting fast, Blair withdrew Southside P's knife. She swung it upward, cutting the mutated rodent in two.

"Darn close call," Julien acknowledged. "Thanks for saving me. Guess you were right; that thing was useful."

Twirling the knife, Blair rolled her eyes. "Yeah, yeah, whatever. Shouldn't we start movin' our asses instead of standin' and lookin' like we haven't got anywhere to be?"

Julien nodded and they speedily traveled farther into the opening. The ceiling lights blinked inconsistently, offering glimpses of its undesirable amenities. Construction equipment lay abandoned. Snuggled under patchy trench coats were a snoring homeless couple. Fragments of electronics were sprinkled in wall corners, some beeping faintly.

"I wish we would've checked the other carts," said Piper. "What if someone was trapped inside with doomsday mice? Theresa was a nice lady. She could be getting eaten."

"They'll have a geet walla more to worry about if we can't catch Navi'el soon, like," Noah vowed.

Blair booted a hardhat out of her path. "I'd prefer to keep goin' and save billions than waste time tryin' to gather up a smaller number. It ain't what ya wanna hear, Piper, but that's the truth. Some gotta die so the rest can live."

"Sucks, but every war has casualties," concurred Julien.

"And here comes the beef," Blair grunted, her pace decelerating.

Puddles ran off the platforms up ahead. A pair of infrared dots danced about one of the station's shallow, beige columns.

"Be quiet and follow my lead," choreographed Julien, flattening his back against the wall.

Collectively, they shimmied into a pocket of shadows.

Theresa came hobbling from the crash's pervasive smog. She had multiple injuries. Her left eye was blackened, and the right dangled loosely. The handkerchief she used to accessorize was doused in tapioca, but not even that clumpy pudding could conceal the cleaved thumb stuck to its overhand knot.

"Help…me…please," she begged.

Eight doomsday mice stormed Theresa, viciously biting her ankles. They dragged the woman toward the shroud of haziness. The Elehominum witnessed her abduction, a mixture of soft whimpers and gnashing teeth haunting them. Piper attempted to spring to Theresa's rescue, but Julien restrained her. A third infrared dot had briefly joined the original two.

"Is someone there? Show yourself, or you'll be sorry. I'm not tawkin' about a slap on the wrist, neither. You'll be cuffed and sent to the slammer for public endangerment," a stern voice demanded via a megaphone.

"We have lifeboats and a shelter in-place. It is our duty to evacuate you safely. Do not be afraid," affirmed a second voice. "The Prime Minister has given us the authority to oversee evacuations."

The men discussed searching bathrooms, but could not decide who would be assigned to the overflowing toilets. Julien awaited the wet sound of their boots stomping away before he spoke.

"American accents, New Yorkers to be exact. I doubt Trump sent any troops, and those dudes definitely aren't British soldiers," he whispered. "You guys thinking what I'm thinking?"

"Heavy footsteps and guns? Gotta be leftover Commandos," presumed Blair.

"Blaxburg wasn't as important as he thought. These nitwits are still functioning without him," mocked Noah.

Piper shook her head. "I knew something stunk worse than us."

"C'mon, we'll get the drop on 'em," Julien incited,

leading the advance.

Tiptoeing out of hiding, the Elehominum scaled the platform to enter the heart of the station. Roof fissures enabled a brewing lightning storm to illuminate the darkened interior. The tan bricks that constructed the building's wall bases were drenched, an ankle-high flood baptizing the walkways. Local Shakespeare play posters were dappled with wet marks. The ink ran, coloring the water opaque.

They took refuge behind a vending machine. Their slow, sloshy footsteps were muffled by the men's continued squabbles. Spying from the vantage point, they clearly identified the supposed rescue officers as frauds. Holding flashlights, both wore black and gray camouflage and gas masks. Unlike their shotgun-wielding peers, however, these two were armed with German Lugers.

The larger of the duo disappeared into the station's Burger King Express, while his big-bellied partner investigated the men's bathroom's outflowing of hand soaps and plungers.

"Bee, you're up first. I want you to shank tubby, but quietly; no smack-talk. Piper's going to be your lookout," planned Julien. "Noah and me will serve his buddy a to-go order. Move when I touch you."

Feeling a tap to her knee, Blair rose and hopped the turnstile. Piper followed four seconds later, taking cover under a ticketing booth desk.

"Kinda like watching an action film," commented Noah. "We *really* are superheroes, mate."

"Nothing fictional here; my scars are real, and so is that knife," Julien replied.

The boys watched Blair stalk the unsuspecting

Commando. He did not detect her clip-clopping strides until it was too late. She stabbed the blade's six-inch length through his carotid artery, slicing up to the base of his gas mask's ear strap. He flumped, causing a big splash.

Piper gave Julien and Noah a thumbs-up.

"Now's our turn. Don't draw any attention to yourself doing something you saw in a movie."

Julien noticed Noah's mischievous smirk as they ducked under the mechanical gate. Proceeding to crouch-walk, they infiltrated the restaurant. An overturned table provided them cover. Their targeted Commando patrolled the kitchen, carelessly spilling cooking supplies. Swaying waters relocated the objects to different sections of the restaurant.

"Where's that sundae pie I stashed?" he caviled.

Julien snatched a frying pan. "We'll sneak closer so you can blind him, then I'll swing."

"Ready when you are," Noah accepted, still smirking.

They rounded the corner, dodging lettuce-filled pots and soggy buns. The Commando had unlatched the freezer, and was unwrapping a packet of fudge when Noah called to him.

"Shouldn't eat that; it'll go straight to your thighs."

The Commando went to unholster his gun, but Noah blew a swirling puff of ectoplasm. The purple, bubbling vapor plastered itself to his goggles. Seizing the opportunity, Julien thwacked him with the frying pan. Sent flying backwards, he slipped on bags of fries and chicken patties.

"A human popsicle, heh? Can't say I want to try it but Emily might've," snickered Noah, shutting the freezer.

Julien secured the latch. "Is that your new thing, puns and one-line zingers?"

"Haven't yi read any comics? Every superhero does 'em," Noah shrugged.

"We aren't superheroes," groaned Julien, walking away.

"How do yi figure we aren't?" Noah contended. "We deserve a show on telly, a three-film deal, and merch. Yeah, lots and lots of merch. Oh, and a multi-player video game, though most people would want to play as me."

They left the Burger King to reconvene with their classmates. Blair looted the Commando's flak jacket, but only found hand-rolled cigars and bubblegum packs. Piper confusingly looked at her reflection in a ticketing booth's window.

"And when were yi gan tell me I'm bald?"

The answer to Piper's question would have to wait. A motorized engine thundered and the waters rippled. Vibrating, the radio attached to the murdered Commando's vest relayed a transmission.

"Fellas, this is Commander MacGregor. What's the status of your sweep? I'll need to report to High Chief Navi'el in thirty. Dun want him to think we're just sitting on our phones."

A chrome jet ski zoomed onto the scene, driven by an unmasked Commando. He had ash-brown hair that was stylized in a pompadour fade. The bottom of his wild ginger beard curved into a single, greasy curl. He sported Celtic cross tattoos on both hands. Patches depicting the flag of Ireland were crookedly stitched onto his jacket's left sleeve.

"Idiots had one job and they still screwed it up," panicked Commander MacGregor, spinning in reverse upon seeing the Elehominum.

Blair jostled to retrieve the dead man's gun, but it was stuck in his holster. After a triumphant tug, she upped it and fired until the clip emptied. Not a single shot landed as the corrupt policeman swerved. Accelerating toward the station's entrance, he drove out to where the flood's waters were far deeper.

Noah spat a beam of violet bubbles at the jet ski's bumper, only for them to pop before connecting. "Crikey, that thing's wicked fast. Reckon it's one of the models we saw them mechanics working on when we got to Noyeur Atlantis."

"Coulda blicked him down if I was quicker," Blair claimed, observing Commander MacGregor's getaway.

Checking the fallen Commando's utility belt, Julien stole a pair of Duracell batteries and a flashlight. He stuffed them into his jumpsuit's pouch.

"Don't stress. We found Blaxburg. We'll find him, too."

Blair chucked the pistol over her shoulder, its heated barrel sizzling in the water. "Oh, look who's finally speakin' to me like he's got some sense. Remembered how to use your big boy words, have ya?"

"Hey, it was my bad for spazzing on you earlier, but you're not going to keep talking crazy to me. Show me the same respect I'm showing you, Bee," ordered Julien.

"And if I don't, what are ya gonna do? Probably whine like a baby," Blair antagonized, poking his forehead.

Noah and Piper forced themselves between the arguing teenagers.

"Don't yi remember what Salvador said, about how Elehominum aren't meant for infighting," Piper prompted, clasping Blair's hands together. "We're not each other's enemies."

Noah patted Julien's chest. "Aye, we can't honor his memory if you two are gan disregard his advice."

Blair's scowl abruptly turned to a look comparable to a strained face during constipation. Doubling, she winced and held her sides.

"Do you want to see if we can find a hospital," asked Julien, shifting past Noah.

"Save your fake concern; I'll be fine," Blair alleged. "Besides, there's a blackout. Ain't gonna let Navi'el's lil' stooges catch me slippin' in some dank waitin' room. These ain't nothin' but cramps before my period. My cycle usually doesn't start 'til the middle of the month, though."

"If that's the kind of pain they bring, I hope mine doesn't ever come," said Piper.

Julien eyed Blair suspiciously. "Seems like it's more than the usual cramps, but you have more experience with periods than me, so I won't push the issue."

After an awkward moment of silence, they left the station.

CHAPTER III

Waves of saltwater rocked outside the train station. The unlit city's damages were momentarily decloaked when lightning flared in the sky. Capsized canoes and paddles coasted from the north, obstructing a halfway-submerged church's exit. Deflated rafts floated lifelessly east of the entrance. Strangely, the westward waters were barely puddles.

"Thank goodness that Commando had this," Julien said, clicking on the flashlight. "Which way will get us to Cumberchester Heights?"

"West, but something's not adding up. How's it the only direction that isn't flooded?" pondered Noah.

Blair rubbed her stomach. "I ain't takin' no chances with swimmin'. It's too dark to see what's below."

They headed west, where sports taverns and hotels were encased in four-sided waterfalls. The moisture fell a centimeter shy of hitting the concrete and was sucked upward, steaming. Stopping in mid stride, Noah marveled at the cycle's repetition. Julien and Piper hooked his arms, pulling him onward.

"What's the big idea? Me legs do work, yi kna!"

"Mhm, I hear you but I'm not letting you stare at

anything for too long. We saw how badly that last curse affected you," Julien explained.

"Aw, hogwash, mate. How'd yi expect I would react to seeing ghosts of me parents?" rationalized Noah. "Cut me some slack; Grimemories are naturally sensitive to magic cuz we're born occultists."

Blair raised her hand to halt the Elehominum's movement. An elderly woman swept kelp off the patio of a charcoal-bricked pub. She was fair-skinned with an afro of kinky, iron-gray curls and full lips. Her eyes were basil-green, and sat behind the lenses of rounded spectacles. The pearls she wore around her wrinkly neck sparkled under the moon's gleam.

"Ma'am, no disrespect, but you shouldn't be outside," Julien warned, noticing the mink robe she donned stopped waist-level to her tight-fitting denim. "With all due respect: nippy weather is the least of your problems."

Standing the broom on its bristles, the woman flashed a smile that showcased her coffee-stained dentures. "You remind me of someone, like a shadow out of time."

"This lady's stark raving mad," judged Noah.

"Jesus, is it impossible for us to meet somebody who ain't a weirdo," Blair sighed, strolling past a trash bin.

"I may be old, but my vision's crisp," said the woman. "You look like him, no ifs, ands, or buts."

Thinking her senile, the graced children followed Blair's lead. They were nearing the end of the street when she spoke again.

"Yes indeed, a spitting image of Jean-Renee. Lordy, do I miss that man."

Julien spun around. "How do you know my great-grandfather?"

"Come inside. I'll answer your question over a cup of tea," the woman assured him, entering the pub.

Intrigued, Julien accepted her offer. Noah and Piper tailed him without a second thought. Blair, however, was as skeptical as ever. She dawdled behind the others, mumbling about their easily-influenced trust.

Freshly baked dough and a slight hint of sweetness scented the airspace. The interior of the pub was lit by wall-mounted candles. A gas-powered stove stood beside a dishwasher. French liqueurs stocked the bar's glass cabinets. Leather couches were positioned at the back-end, near a curtained section. The hardwood floor was a blend of browns and reds, with skillfully cut and varnished grooves between the planks.

"I don't mean to be rude, but I asked you a question: who are you, and how do you know my great-grandfather?"

Dropping sugar cubes into four teacups, the woman set out spoons. "Ah, Jean-Renee. Yes, he was a special gentleman. In fact, he was the first person I met when I came to Newcastle. As for my name, you may call me Madam Marie."

"Were you friends, or something more?" Julien questioned, stirring his drink.

"We were lovebugs, yeah," certified Madam Marie. "He was a helluva lot older than me, but so doggone handsome. The age difference bothered him, not me.

In the end, my Cajun charm got him."

A microwave behind the bar buzzed.

Madam Marie turned and bent over, retrieving a cup of hot chocolate. Julien focused on the round imprint of her hindquarters.

Blair fanned steam from her drink. "Since someone's obviously too horny to ask, I will: how did you meet Julien's great-grandfather?"

"My daddy gave me a loan to start a business," Madam Marie said, topping her drink with whipped cream. "I opened two brothels here in Newcastle. Jean-Renee stopped by one and we had a chat. He was saying my gals deserved the chance to be more than hookers. I told him I'd change my business on one condition: he had to keep coming to see me."

Disgusted, Blair sent her cup to the end of the counter. "I ain't gonna put my lips on nothin' some random thot's drank outta."

"I beg your pardon, missy," snapped Madam Marie. "I'll have you know that was many moons ago, and my dishes are always washed thoroughly. Lacroque is one of Newcastle's most reputable businesses."

Noah rose from his stool and approached a jukebox. "Sorry, I get that Julien wants to know all about his great-grandfather, but I have a concern of my own: why isn't your pub like the others we saw?"

"Jean-Renee taught me a few voodoo spells to protect my possessions," denuded Madam Marie. "But there were some things he could do that me nor anybody else could."

"How did you find out?" Julien questioned.

"I wondered how a colored man became so wealthy," said Madam Marie. "One windy night, when he left the pub drunk, I had my driver follow him to Cumberchester Heights. You can imagine my surprise when I saw him turn a rock into a gold key that unlocked his front door."

"And then what?" Julien pestered.

Madam Marie licked away the creamy residue on her upper lip. "Jean-Renee had been aware of my car the entire time. He invited me in and explained everything. The school, his powers, you name it. It was like hearing an angel talk about their good works on Earth. Suffice to say, I was smitten. He trusted me to keep his secrets and when he realized that I would, he was more amenable to us having a relationship."

"So, you're kinda like Julien's great-grandmother in a way," said Piper.

"That might be somewhat of a stretch. My surname is still Bordeaux because he never married me," Madam Marie asserted. "Mind you, he wanted to. We had plans to have a wedding in Paris days before he died."

"No one's ever told me how he passed," admitted Julien.

Noah grinned, selecting a jazz-funk instrumental. "Howay, something interesting. Enough of this romantic rubbish; let's hear about how the bloke went out in a blaze of glory!"

Julien, Blair, and Piper looked at him with scrunched up facial expressions.

"What's got everyone's knickers in a twist," Noah asked. "Death's awesome; don't act like you lot didn't expect me, a Grimemory, to wanna hear these deets."

Madam Marie stirred her drink. "Unless essential, I don't discuss unpleasant matters."

"Julien deserves to know," argued Blair, slamming her fist onto the counter.

"Yee, he does," Piper piggybacked.

"Please, it's part of my family's history," urged Julien. "I'd appreciate you telling me."

Madam Marie closed her eyes and exhaled. "One of the cultists he fought was strong, and I mean real strong. Jean-Renee couldn't manage to kill her, so he did something unforgivable."

"Which was what?" questioned Julien.

"He combined the powers of his grace with an old Haitian curse, and used them to trap her inside a metal amulet. Therein lies the problem: curses aren't a one-way street. In order for her to stay imprisoned, years would have to be taken off his life. It was bound to happen," Madam Marie detailed.

"Brutal," Noah said, reclaiming his seat at the bar.

"I had to watch him fight every illness you can think of," elaborated Madam Marie. "Doctors were dumbfounded by his symptoms. Most thought he had some rare form of the bubonic plague, while others were convinced it was a combination of cancers. His official cause of death was acute respiratory failure."

Julien was silent, absentmindedly straggling toward the curtained domain.

"I am sorry for upsetting you, but you wanted to know," Madam Marie apologized.

"No, it's not that," said Julien. "I'm just having a hard time understanding why that would be unforgivable."

"The Celortus wouldn't want an Elehominum using dark magic, and that goes double for some that might've been inspired by the Mavkardia," reasoned Piper.

"Heretikrox," Noah uttered.

"Lovely, more words I dunno the definition of," groaned Blair.

"It's an Old Celortian word for the process of mixing something pure with something vile, and only a person well-trained in sorcery can pull it off," Noah explicated. "Yi need the blood of a newborn for everything to work properly."

"Wait, you're telling me that my great-grandfather killed a...?" Julien paused, unable to complete his sentence.

A convection oven below the microwave ticked.

Madam Marie pulled out a baking sheet that held loaves of banana bread. "Y'all probably could use a bite to eat. I'm certain full bellies will take your minds off this unnecessary ugliness."

"You ain't too keen on talkin' bout this. That wouldn't be cuz ya got something to hide, would it?" speculated Blair.

"Absolutely not," Madam Marie said. "I simply do not think it is healthy for youngins to ponder such dark things."

"She's right, we should leave it be. How would Jean-Renee even know how to do heretikrox?" advocated Piper, grabbing a slice of bread.

Noah sipped his tea. "Hmm, good question. I suppose he could've read up on it in the Restricted Area of the Library of Solstice. I remember finding a book there with step-by-step instructions."

"Father Nigel and Sister Agnieszka wouldn't be okay with yi reading that; you're supposed to get permission before even going inside," shamed Piper.

"Chillax, I didn't get very far," Noah claimed, biting

a corner of her bread. "I was bored one night and got curious, so I snuck in. I had nearly finished reading the first step before Solomon caught me."

"Who the hell's Solomon?" asked Blair.

"He's a timekeeper," Noah answered. "The Celortus created him to guard our school's more sensitive records in the Library of Solstice."

"And to not make it easy for Elehominum like yi to snoop where they divvent belong," added Piper.

"You're sayin' that, regardless of whether or not I've got the Electromni, there's still places I'm not allowed into," questioned Blair.

"The Electromni is your key to enter the chambers reserved for a Gelectrika, just like how the Scarlet Gospels let me enter the chambers reserved for a Grimemory," Noah explained. "The Restricted Area is a different ballgame. It's hidden behind a bookcase, and won't open for anyone that doesn't know what they're doing."

"Ya hear that, bruv? My lil' electric scroll is as worthless as that big metal book of yours," Blair said to Julien, who was staring at the pub's more exclusive zone.

"Yi areet, mate? Yi haven't blinked once," inquired Noah.

Julien took a deep breath. "What're these curtains hiding?"

"Mo' quizzical than my daddy's old cat, just like your great-grandpappy," Madam Marie sighed. "I'm a legitimate businesswoman, and normally wouldn't let anyone make demands of me. In this case, I feel obligated to oblige."

The gray-haired mistress left her position, and

sauntered to the pub's private subsection. She took hold of the tilt wand, tearing back the curtains to unveil a collection of personal treasures.

A sofa autographed by countless jazz icons such as Louis Armstrong, Duke Ellington, and Ella Fitzgerald was pressed against a cedarwood wall. Framed pictures of Jean-Renee and Madam Marie hung on that same wall.

"Look at him, so happy and full of life," mused Julien, noting his great-grandfather's laughing expression in the largest portrait of the assortment. "You'd never guess he was fighting a terminal illness, let alone monsters."

Madam Marie smiled, caressing the right edge of the frame. "Jean-Renee had a poker-face like you wouldn't believe. He'd be in agony, and not make one peep about it."

"Where was this one taken?" asked Julien, referring to a photograph that depicted a medieval cathedral.

"The Cathedral Church of St. Nicholas, where many wanderers find their soulmates. He was the patron saint of sailors and boats, you know," Madam Marie stated. "Jean-Renee was in so much pain that day. He didn't have the strength to hold the camera up properly. I had to stand behind him and angle his hands, which is why neither of us is in the shot."

"Me and mam go there for the Christmas services every year. It's the prettiest place in the city center," said Piper.

"Can't see my great-grandfather hanging in churches. The men on my dad's side of the family have been atheists for a long time," Julien muttered.

"You're getting ahead of yourself, mon chéri. I

never said we were going inside. Me and him were admiring the architecture and dedication of man hours that went into designing it," corrected Madam Marie. "And Jean-Renee wasn't a pure atheist. He placed his faith in the Celortus, and the divinity of Earth's elements."

"In that case, him doing heretikrox makes tuns of sense. They say there's only two types who have the nerve to do it: the passionate and the power-hungry," Noah said.

"And who are *they*? Let me guess: they're the older Elehominum that were bumbling around the Restricted Section, aye," deprecated Piper. "Yi sure do know how to pick your role models."

"Hey, they might've broken a few rules, but it was all in the name of good old-fashioned research," Noah contested. "We're Wolven scholars for a reason. No shame in wanting to learn about the history of our world."

"Gang nem's so busy speculatin' on man's work, they ain't pree what's beside the couch," interjected Blair.

Less than four inches from the furniture's cotton-spewing armrest was a medium-sized copper pedestal. It supported a square object that was obscured by a pink quilt.

Madam Marie stepped protectively in front of the conspicuous stanchion. "I'm beginning to feel as though my kindness is being taken for weakness. An old woman's privacy should be respected."

"But you ain't got nothin' to hide. Shouldn't be too hard to show us what's underneath the cover," Blair suggested, sliding off her stool.

"I've shown you children the greatest hospitality, but I will not be bullied into doing something I'm uncomfortable with," maintained Madam Marie.

Feigning interest in a photograph of Jean-Renee on a bicycle, Noah ambled over to the pedestal. Snatching off the quilt, he uncloaked the mystery. Housed inside a glass crate was a wrinkled, dark brown tube-like structure. Its edges were concave and crispy, similar to overcooked bacon strips.

"All this fuss about an old piece of meat," Blair sneered.

"Are you blind?" blurted Julien, inspecting the contents. "That isn't food; it's an umbilical cord."

Blair's lips quivered and her knees buckled. Belching, she doubled and vomited green gushes onto the floor. Piper came to her aid, patting her back and offering a cup of water.

"We've seen plenty of gross junk, especially in Noyeur Atlantis. Who'd have thunk this would make her lose her lunch?" Noah contemplated.

Yanking the quilt from him, Madam Marie dabbed at the marshy residue smeared along the corners of Blair's mouth.

"You had quite the extreme reaction, suga. I won't beat around the bush: I don't believe it was the sight of an umbilical cord that caused you to vomit. Is there a chance you could be pregnant?"

"Hell nah there's not. Last person I had sex with was…," Blair hesitated, her eyes fleetingly meeting Julien's. "I ain't knocked up. End of story."

"I said much the same, days before the tests confirmed I most certainly was going through my first pregnancy. If you are, I got an inkling the daddy will prove himself worthwhile," predicted Madam Marie.

The scientific findings from Dr. Jung's hologram presentation reoccurred in Julien's mind. He remembered him stating that a child conceived by two Elehominum parents would rapidly mature inside the mother's womb. He sweated, and sought to shift the conversation's focus.

"So, uh, is this cord from your oldest baby?"

"My youngest," informed Madam Marie, her tone lowering. "I was well past my prime when I was pregnant with him. The physicians told me to get an abortion, but I thought it was a miracle. I did my best to stay healthy while carrying him for those nine months. I went as far as hiring a dietician and a personal trainer. My efforts were moot; I gave birth to a stillborn. His name was Pierre."

"I'm sorry. That's so sad," said Piper.

"Now, now, lil' wun. Don't pity me; accidents can happen when a person fights biology. We need to find out if your friend is a mama to be," Madam Marie redirected, pressing the back of her hand to Blair's forehead to check her temperature. "Honey, do you remember your last period?"

Noah clamped both hands over his ears. "Yuck! Who wants to hear this madness about lasses bleeding rivers and releasing cruddy eggs, like? The smell alone must be downright putrid. How do yi bleed for days, and not die?"

Hearing his immature explanation of menstruation, Blair vomited again.

"Way to go, Noah. You can be a real butt-head sometimes," admonished Piper.

"Quit being so insensitive, boy. Maybe a chore or two will teach you some respect. Go make yourself useful, and clean up," Madam Marie commanded, pointing at a mop and soap-filled bucket near the pub's entrance.

Noah mumbled under his breath, but did as he was told.

"I think it's best that we allow her a moment's rest," Madam Marie said to Julien. "I have a few vacant rooms upstairs, if anyone else would like to take a nap."

"We don't want to inconvenience you. Besides, who knows if it's an actual pregnancy? It could just be a bug. She can probably walk it off," replied a nervous Julien, his words lacking conviction.

Guzzling the water, Blair flopped onto a folding chair. "I'm fine. My stomach is probably just playin' up cuz of something I ate in Noyeur Atlantis."

"Aw, yee, that reminds me: while the three of yi went to the Forlorn Shrine, I was chowing on tender steak cutlets," said Noah, scrubbing the floor clean of disgorged stomach matter. "And don't get me started on the mash with onion gravy. So tasty!"

Blair vomited a third time, splattering a suede footrest and the tips of Madam Marie's slippers.

Noah dropped the mop in frustration. "Are yi serious? I haven't finished cleaning the first two puke puddles, and you're already blowing your guts again. If there is a baby in there, I'd better be made the godfather for all the cleaning I'm already doing!"

"She's in denial. I've been pregnant enough times to recognize the signs," Madam Marie whispered, wrapping her arm around Julien's neck as she guided him toward the bar. "I want you to be honest: do you know who is the daddy?"

"I have an idea of who it could be, yeah, but I'm not entirely sure," said Julien.

"Well, I'll be damned. I guess it ain't just her that's denying the obvious," said Madam Marie, using a washrag to dab Julien's sweaty nose. "Your left nostril gets wet when you lie, just like Jean-Renee's."

CHAPTER IV

etergent and hot bleach rinsed away the nasty splatters. Soap bubbles coated Lacroque's main floor, following Noah as he mopped the tiles to a glister. Piper busied herself at a pinstriped booth, chopping lemons to be put into Blair's refilled glass. Julien stuffed his face with bread, thinking a mouthful of food would save him from further paternity questioning.

"This should make you feel better," Madam Marie said, laying a cold compress across Blair's forehead. "I wish you four would listen to reason, and sleep for a lil' while."

Julien wiped crumbs off his lips. "You're sweet, and we're grateful for your generosity, but time's not exactly on our side."

"Mummies need rest," prescribed Piper, walking the drink over to Blair. "Me mam says there's two things yi can never have enough of: rest and Flintstone vitamins."

"And in this case, a puke pail," Noah fussed.

Downing the lemon-enriched water, Blair removed the wet rag from her forehead. "Nobody here's a doctor, so let's dead the baby talk, yeah? If it'd make everyone shut up, I'll grab a pregnancy test later. Keyword: later. I'm ready to go whack Navi'el now."

"Should probably grab a DNA test while you're at it," berated Julien.

Blair dropped her glass, lemons and shards splashing into the suds. "What did you say?"

"Nothing, dude. For the kid's sake, I just hope your goofball ex-boyfriend isn't the dad," Julien responded.

"You're braindead if ya believe I'm still lettin' him smash," seethed Blair, throwing the damp rag at him. "The only person I've been with in months is you."

Noah stopped mopping, his amber eyes wide with shock. Piper, who had been picking up the spilled fruits, ceased her janitorial efforts to watch the oldest Elehominum argue.

"Maybe I'd buy that if I hadn't heard your voice change once you recognized that dirtbag," Julien proposed.

"It's honestly crazy how insecure you can be," accosted Blair. "I was surprised, not smitten. You'd be able to tell the difference if you had more experience with real girls, and not just the ones on your computer screen."

"Yeah, because I should totally take tips from a chick who hangs in the ghetto with illiterate troublemakers. Wonder how much *experience* they gave you?" Julien bickered, shaking his head.

Blair stepped closer, her kneecaps emitting sparks. "Ya been beggin' for this smoke. I got what ya need."

"I'd like to see you try. You can't beat me, I'm the one who's been saving our skins when the chips are down," said Julien.

"Quiet, the both of you," enjoined Madam Marie, maneuvering between the quarreling teenagers. "There will be no roughhousing or wrasslin' in my pub, you hear?"

"Aight, tell little boy Preux to meet me outside then," Blair demanded, departing Lacroque.

Chasing after her, Piper listed off the de-stress exercises her mother found most beneficial. Upon hearing the suggestion of prayer, Noah slid the bucket out of his way.

"I'd better go stop her from mentioning those silly breathing methods."

In his rush to end Piper's yoga-centric preaching, Noah tripped over a raised floorboard. He fell onto his hands and knees, catching himself on the mop's yarn strings. Leveraging his weight, he regained an upright posture.

"That has to be a violation of safety regulations," he said, halfway through the door. "I'd fix it fast if I were yi. Someone could really hurt themselves, and I'm sure yi don't wanna get sued by some pleb looking for a come-up."

Julien went to follow Noah, but Madam Marie blocked his path.

"Jean-Renee would be turning in his grave if he heard how you spoke to that gal. You owe her an apology."

"Why would I apologize? You saw how she was acting. Seemed flat-out guilty to me."

"In your heart of hearts, do you reckon she has any reason to lie to you?"

The thought skirted through Julien's mind like an out-of-control racecar. He harkened back to their initial meeting, recalling her disclosures of surviving ovarian cancer and poverty in Southwark. Sighing, he lowered his head in acknowledgement of wrongdoing.

"You're still learning about life," Madam Marie counseled, taking his hands into her own. "Everyone makes mistakes. Ain't too late for you to admit you screwed up."

"You have a point. My jealousy got the best of me," conceded Julien.

Unlinking their hands, Madam Marie shifted to the spot where Noah tripped. "Before you leave, I want to give you something."

"I wouldn't feel right taking anything from you, not after the scene Bee and I caused. You've already given us food and drinks," refused Julien.

Reaching under the floorboard, Madam Marie procured a star-shaped amulet. It was super-black in color, and fit with a tarnished gold chain. Its Cuban links stunk of gunpowder.

"This was what Jean-Renee used to entrap the cultist," she divulged. "He wanted me to keep it safe, so I buried it here with my rifles. Came home from my vacation in Louisiana this morning, and saw the floorboard had been dug up."

Julien shook his head in disbelief. "But that means…"

"The hussy escaped, yup," Madam Marie verified, handing Julien the amulet. "I won't lie to you: getting her back inside won't be no cakewalk. The upside is, if anybody can, they'll be one of Jean-Renee's kin."

"But she can't die. She's a combat vet, probably knows every trick in the book," freighted Julien.

"You're a Preux; nobody's smarter than you gents,"

Madam Marie winked.

"Welp, being pessimistic won't do me any good," said Julien, pocketing the eldritch artifact. "I'll put your theory to the test when the heat's on. In the meantime, I have an apology to make."

Madam Marie removed her glasses, and used the sleeves of her robe to buff the lenses. She then observed his walk toward the door, offering a cryptic word of advice.

"Be careful; out there be monsters."

Stars loomed in the dark curtain of velvet that was the sky, as if strung in the air by invisible wires. Blair's profanity-laced ramblings loudened the otherwise quiet night. She paced angrily, swinging her arms and wishing that Julien would be bold enough to repeat himself.

Noah and Piper tried to talk the ill-tempered girl down, mindful of her previous overload and eventual loss of consciousness. They failed miserably.

"Man must've gone cuckoo, chattin' tough to me. I'm really on drills," Blair ranted. "He's lucky I ain't got none of them Commandos' guns, cuz it's a mad 'ting if I press that trigger."

Making his presence known, Julien closed the door to Lacroque behind him. "Hey, guys. I wanted to say I'm sorry for the way I acted. I could've handled the situation much better."

"Bruv, I ain't forgivin' nothin'," Blair reproached, tipping over an outdoor ashtray. "You tried to make it seem like I'm easy cuz I'm from the 'hood. Your words don't mean jack to me."

"I can't blame you for being upset. You have every right to be, but I want you to know that I'll do what's necessary to get us past this," said Julien.

"Don't cop a plea now. After we waste Navi'el, I'm gonna check your chin," Blair guaranteed.

"We'll cross that road when we get there," decided Julien. "Our main priority is getting to Cumberchester Heights. Buses probably aren't being driven in a blackout, at least not home in the States. We'll have to go on foot."

They resumed their westward tour. The buildings at the end of the street, unlike their counterparts, were not encased in four-sided waterfalls. Instead, each was showered by its own raincloud that slowly boiled the roof foundations.

"Sea monsters, sunken civilizations, supernatural floods," Julien catalogued, stopping at a vintage sports store. "The Bible might not have been fiction."

The Elehominum beheld the inexplicable destruction, marveling as gutters and vents were cooked without so much as a simmer. The demonic shrills of a motor stole their attention. Jumping a mound of toppled telephone booths on the street's right side, Commander MacGregor fired a slew of bullets from a Luger. He hit the store's welcome sign and front window, missing Noah's shoulder by half an inch. The glass shattered synchronically with his chrome jet ski landing on a water current.

"I want everyone inside, hurry," rallied Julien. "Find the backdoor and stake it out. Don't let anyone get too close."

Noah and Piper obeyed his orders, sprinting

through the shard-crowned opening.

Blair stepped in halfway, and tossed Julien a soccer ball. Before he could thank her for the assist, she disappeared behind aisles of cricket gear.

"Playing hero now was pretty thick. Should've ran with your mates so the four of ya'd die together," Commander MacGregor lambasted, reloading his pistol.

Julien chucked the ball at his hands, forcing him to drop the gun. It let off one shot, and swiftly sank beneath the shaded waves.

"Ah, no worries, laddie; there's plenty more toys where that one came from. We'll play shoot 'em up soon," threatened Commander MacGregor, revving his engine and fleeing.

Julien watched the jet ski blitz ahead, its silvery body becoming a perishing light in the distance. Liquid nitrogen was funneled through its needle-nosed nozzles, producing a smoky eruption upon contact with the water. Once the Irish Commando had fully vanished, he entered the store.

Inside was a minefield for the clumsy. Emptied yet generating blank receipts, a cash register was at the very edge of a slippery tabletop. Delicate, hand-crafted rugby figurines, sat on low shelves where they could be easily knocked and damaged. Posters of famous British boxers like Lennox Lewis and Anthony Joshua were pinned to the walls with thumbtacks, their corners creased and unsecured.

Other, less valuable sports memorabilia shared the wide, single-floored establishment. Scattered boxes along the rubber floor held ring-worn singlets of amateur Scottish wrestlers, teapots sculpted to look like American footballs, and whistles blown in Newcastle United Football Club scrimmages.

"Dad would lose his mind if he saw how much merch they've got," Julien said, wandering the cricket aisles. "Wonder if he'll believe me when I say I didn't get him anything because I was too busy preventing human extinction."

Seeking the backdoor Noah and Piper were instructed to find, he bumped into a container partially concealed by the store's lack of lighting. Aiming the flashlight downward, he identified it as a drink cooler. He popped the lid and took an armful of four lukewarm, grape-flavored Gatorades.

"Sucks the store has no power to keep these chilled. Oh well, they'll hydrate us all the same," determined Julien, straightening his hunched posture. "Where the heck's that backdoor?"

The clatter of wood cracking sounded ten feet to the left of him. Shining the light onto a rack of weightlifting belts, he located the secondary exit and scuttled through the ajar doorway into an alley.

Broken baseball bat in-hand, Blair stepped over an incapacitated Commando. Noah and Piper dragged him to an iron fence, and handcuffed him to the post. He wallowed in blood and sawdust.

"What, was this bozo standing guard or something?" Julien asked.

"Seems he had a mind to, yee," said Noah. "We saw him looking around the trashcans, whinging about how he'd ran outta bullets. He heard me breathe, but didn't have a chance to buck. The bloke had his noggin beat like an egg for Sunday breakfast. Scrambled 'em up good."

"Aye, anotha radgie gadgie doon, and it was one of the cleanest swings I've ever seen," Piper graded, dropping the handcuff key down a storm drain.

Julien handed them both a Gatorade. "Their numbers are decreasing, but we shouldn't get cocky. Me and MacGregor's run-in ended with him hightailing it. Navi'el's giving him orders, so they've got a plan in place. Let's make sure we're on our Ps and Qs."

Relinquishing what remained of the splintered bat, Blair stole a Gatorade from him. She removed the cap and drank voraciously, guzzling the purple beverage in seconds. The empty bottle was thrown at the Commando's gas mask to add insult to his injury.

"This alley will take us farther into the city center," said Noah. "We can get to Edenshire in forty-five minutes if we hustle. Course, it'll be a wee bit longer if we hav'ta fight anybody else."

Blair reached into her skirt's pocket and retrieved a Chicago Bulls bandana, masking herself. "No complaints here. Bally up, spot man, and get splashy."

"Erm, I'm assuming that means Bee is ready to handle business. I don't have any objections to that," Julien interpreted, directing their trip to the alley's exitway.

They marched along the cobbled pavement. Aspen leaves and beer caps crunched beneath their footsteps.

"I feel for you, bro," giggled Noah, striding to Julien's left. "You're American. Can't be easy listening to two Geordies and a London road girl talk. I'd be proppa lost, like. Bet you'd kill for subtitles."

To his right, Piper sipped her Gatorade. "Everybody knows Scousers have the thickest accents in the UK. Geordies aren't hard to understand. He'd tell us if we were."

"Are you mental? When's the last time yi met an American that knew what a *netty* is," Noah disputed.

Julien paid no heed to the debating duo. He engrossed himself with monitoring Blair's behavior. She regularly rubbed her stomach, subtly wincing every so often. He had been so taken by his study of her that he walked straight into a tattered mattress.

"How dee yi expect us to be watchful if yi won't dee the same" predicated Noah, steadying him at the hips. "Not trying to be a smart aleck, but what if that was a board of nails, or a ginormous woodchipper?"

Piper dusted Julien's jumpsuit clean of lint. "Get real. Who'd put those in an alley?"

"Hey, anything's possible. A few weeks ago, I saw a kid and his dog playing fetch with lawnmower plugs in Arthur's Hill," Noah said.

"Reet, in Arthur. If yi haven't gotten the memo, I'll tell yi again: we're in the city center," resolved Piper, readjusting the slanted front pouch of Julien's jumpsuit. "The crazies keep to themselves. They wouldn't be 'round these parts long before the police found them meddling in mess."

Blair stood at the alley's end, a dim flicker of blueness illuminating her face. "Ya might've spoken too soon, cuz the crazies are in full effect."

Julien, Noah, and Piper joined her in observance of a bizarre sight. Sky-reaching walls of water bracketed them, blocking every unexplored direction but north. A sudden, violent gust of wind pushed them across the street, where they arrived at a carnival dead center in the cluster of Newcastle's most historical buildings.

Accordion music played in the distance, courtesy of a band perched on a 131-foot column tower. Clowns wearing glow in the dark makeup biked on unicycles around a white marble statue of Queen Victoria, juggling rotten tomatoes. Two hunchbacked men sparred with replica lightsabers to entertain a crowd of children. Buxom women painted to resemble cheetahs strolled along circus tents, giving free cotton candy to drunken attendees.

A gargantuan steel sculpture of an angel overlooked the extravaganza. Flaming trapezes were appended to its wings, which were seemingly angled to create a sense of embrace. Performers in spandex bikinis swung from one side to the other, their bodies spinning like human tornadoes.

"Can't say I'd consider this to be the ideal time of year for a county fair, but maybe stuff's different in England," said Julien. "Then again, there's always a chance that this is more sheisty than what it appears."

"Something's really wrong," stated Piper, trashing her Gatorade in a recycling bin.

"How can you tell?" Julien asked.

"These landmarks are displaced. Certain ones, yi wouldn't even see unless yi walked farther," co-signed Noah, drinking the last of his Gatorade. "It's like the entire county's being warped."

Blair pie-faced a drunkard that stumbled too close to the group. "Timeout: did I hear that correctly? If reality is legit gettin' mucked up, I don't see how you can be sure we're still movin' right."

"If being an Elehominum has taught me anything, it's that nothing's for sure," Noah said. "The safest bet is to keep heading straight, but I get what you're saying; not knowing where we're going could be disastrous."

"We'll stick to the original plan. Keep your eyes open. I want constant vigilance," mandated Julien.

They crept deeper into the city center's nucleus. Fishy smells became dominant. Manned by cooks who wore lightbulbs on their aprons, food stands offering deformed seafood and ice cream combinations sat in abundance. Those serving three-eyed flounder heads, topped with two scoops of freezer-burnt vanilla, garnered the longest lines.

"We've just passed some of my neighbors. They'd never eat somewhere that isn't kosher," Piper notified. "They've been bewitched."

"Yi can bet Navi'el is working overtime. No telling what else the bastard's done," presupposed Noah.

Julien paused at a bronze statue of Dr. Martin Luther King Jr. "How about taking a Civil Rights memorial for starters?"

"Mate, believe it or not, this is property of Newcastle Uni," Noah annotated. "They gave MLK an honorary degree in 1967, and he visited to receive it in-person."

"Man was fearless. Got up every damn day, and never quit his fight. That's gangsta," said Blair, staring into the statue's resolute eyes.

A contrabass clarinet resounded behind the Elehominum.

"She has been expecting you four."

CHAPTER V

A boy with hyperpigmented brown skin stood guard at an orange and white striped tent. He had severe spinal curvature, and was bowlegged. Two black mambas slithered about the waistline of his long, purple paisley-patterned dashiki. A third one coiled his neck, its dark blue tongue lovingly licking the crevices of his inner ear.

"Who has been expecting us?" Julien questioned.

"We ain't make no reservations, so what could any of these freaks want with us except trouble?" said Blair.

The sound of their voices frenzied the snakes. Hissing, they skated to the ground and flexed their cobra-like neck flaps. The reptilian trio charged forth, but froze as their owner played the clarinet. Retreating, each of the predators calmly reclaimed their positions on him.

"She," the boy repeated, opening the tent's burlap curtain. "If it's answers you seek, step inside. The lady's time is so very precious."

"He's a snake charmer. They're not exactly the type to be trusted," whispered Noah to Julien.

"Had my intentions been bad, I would have

allowed my pets to strike," the boy insisted. "I am but a good Samaritan, who lives to serve, and serves to live. Such is the will of my master."

Piper leaned in closer for a better look at the fangs of the bottommost snake. "He has a point. Those mambas are scary critters. Me mam says one bite is enough to kill a grownup."

"I'll tell you what: if you can give me a reason why you think us, out of all the people here tonight, need answers, we'll trust you. Otherwise, my friends and I aren't interested," Julien propounded.

"And no paranormal quotes or proverbs are gonna cut it. We only want facts," haggled Blair.

"Edenshire Academy's faculty has not been completely truthful with you. The four of you wouldn't have known who Emily Harper was had you not found and attacked her," the boy said, turning to Julien. "Doesn't that make you wonder what they could've chosen not to tell you about your great-grandfather?"

"The last person that dissed our envoys got bodied, so watch them crusty lips, aight," exhorted Blair.

"Besides, yi didn't write their lecture plans. Emily and other topics might've been planned for a certain month," Noah said. "Sounds like you're chatting outta your bum, if I'm honest."

"They always had a good reason for what they did," attested Piper.

Julien held back his classmates. "We take our school very seriously. Snakes or no snakes, an outsider making people we care about out to be liars isn't going to do anything but make us match that energy."

"Understandable. I live to spread the knowledge

my service earns me. I did not mean to come across so harshly. Forgive my manic passion," the boy supplicated, bowing his head. "But there is more you should know. I humbly ask you to speak with my master."

Julien thought back to his heated discussion with Salvador. He had slandered the Vulcanold's religious faith in favor of sciences. The argument ended when Piper, along with Ava, explained that neither were wrong for their convictions. It was intolerance of each other's viewpoints that almost soured a crucial moment of clarity.

"Everyone makes mistakes. Heck, I put my foot in my mouth often," Julien sympathized, shepherding the Elehominum inside. "Just try to be a little more respectful of our school."

Noah's eyes curiously appraised the boy's clarinet as he entered first. Piper dallied in behind him. Infinitely less prudent than her classmates, Blair stepped into the boy's personal space.

"I ain't the one for forgiveness. As far as I'm concerned, we should've beat you for what you said. Play crazy again and there won't be passes or pardons," she pledged, ignoring a strike-ready snake.

Wary of the angered predator, Julien placed one hand on the small of Blair's back and the other on her elbow. She promptly shook him off and entered the tent. He babbled variations of his original apology, following her like a lovesick puppy.

The tent stored plastic bottles of multi-colored carbonated liquids. Arranged in the order of biggest to smallest, they furnished the ten shelves of a tall, acacia bookcase that spanned the shelter's square footage. Each bubbly concoction was labeled with a name written on a strip of aluminum tape. All appeared to be Germanic in origin, save for a corked one full of a colorless substance.

Julien had discontinued his plea bargaining to Blair. He opted to inspect the materials set on a cement table, using a floating kerosene lantern to maximize the efforts of his study. Disorganized tarot cards bordered a crystal ball. A bowl of salt and ashes harbored two white sage sticks.

"Pretty lame joke for him to play, telling us there's someone here when there isn't," Piper pouted.

"He's probably a has-been illusionist wantin' some cheap oohs and aahs," said Blair.

"Na, whoever is that lad's master has a serious collection of potions," Noah enthusiastically evaluated, stalking the shelves. "Bloody hell, they've got Veritaseru…"

"Do not finish zee name. I vent to a secret castle in zee Scottish Highlands to acquire it, and I am offended zat you dare speak of its existence," a growly voice next to Julien interrupted.

The lantern's bearer was revealed to be a gray woman in a lace wedding dress and matching opera gloves. She wore her white hair in a high side ponytail. Her top lip was painted matte teal, while her bottom was nude but pierced with a diamond stud. In place of eyebrows, she had two exposed bone structures that formed an M.

Startled, Julien backed into Noah. "Would it kill you to give us a warning before you appear out of thin air?"

"Jumpy, are ve?" the gray woman taunted, sitting the lantern on the table. "Calm your nerves. You do not vant to die of a heart attack."

"My health's none of your concern. We're here to get the answers your manservant says you've got," said Julien.

"Ah, yes. He is but a simple Persian boy in search of visdom," the gray woman nodded. "I have vhat you desire. Pick a card, any vill suffice."

"Ya can't be for real. Ya think we want our fortunes told, when there's a supernatural flood ragin'?" snorted Blair, knocking the crystal ball to the ground.

The mystical tool fragmented on impact. Remarkably, it reassembled and returned to the table. The edges of the tarot cards then became razored. Levitating, the deck shuffled itself in Blair's face.

"You vill not do zat again," the gray woman governed.

Julien carefully drew a card with his thumb and index finger. "We didn't come looking for a fight. If we have to pick cards to get answers, no prob, that's what we'll do."

Pictured on the squared cut of cotton-paper was the image of a house mouse cowering in a desert pothole.

"Impending Doom," clarified the gray woman, perusing a row of potions. "Zis is not good. I vant to help you. Unfortunately, zee cards tell no lies and zey cannot be defied. Doing so vould be an affront to nature, and zat is unacceptable."

"Can I go next? Maybe mine'll be better," Piper nagged.

"Not to rain on anyone's parade, but let's not get sidetracked," reaffirmed Julien. "If you can't tell us anything worthwhile about our school or how to stop what's happening, say that and we'll be on our way."

The gray woman selected a spiraled bottle. "Yes, I am familiar vith Edenshire Academy. Very intimately."

"Somebody needs to let this bitch know we ain't interested in story buildup," Blair spurred.

"So impatient," said the gray woman, removing her left glove. "I've been gone for so long. Allow me to indulge in zis decadent moment."

Noah gasped and his eyes grew wide with insight. "We should leave. Now."

"But I'd like my fortune read, too," Piper harped.

"Forget the reading," wailed Noah.

The gray woman tore off the bottom half of her dress, uncovering a long pair of scaly legs.

"She is…she's…she's," Noah stammered.

"What's gotten into you," asked Julien.

"Spit it out," Blair entreated, shaking Noah by his shoulders.

Unscrewing the bottle's cap, the gray woman bathed in a blue-black fluid. Her naked arm twitched and mutated into an elongated bayonet that oozed the potion's color. Its tip exuded vinegary fumes. Both of her legs merged, becoming a singular, slithering limb. She had reached the height of six feet.

"His great-grandfather's trinket binds me no longer. Say my name."

"She's Klara von Schlange," publicized Noah breathlessly.

The devilish crossbreed gashed a hole in the tent's tarpaulin ceiling, basking beneath the light of a red moon. Her nose compressed, and her nostrils were reduced to diagonal slits.

"Run," Julien shrieked.

The Elehominum stampeded out of the tent. Attempting to thwart their escape, the snake-charming boy leapt in front of them. The mambas he wielded wormed their way up to his shoulders and penetrated his ears. He convulsed as they writhed under the now-crackling skin of his face and neck.

Julien swung the flashlight, leveling him with a precise blow to the temple.

"Keep moving, don't stop until we leave the city center," he dictated, stomping the snake charmer's clarinet.

They ran, pushing past scores of carnival goers. Their team sprint, however, was stalled when Blair slipped and fell on glow sticks. Gnarled asphalt abraded her knees.

"Try to be more careful," said Julien, extending his hand.

Blair snubbed the offer. "Sorry I haven't got any eyes on my bunions."

"Don't look now, but we've got company," Noah communicated.

The snake charmer was heading straight for them. Two mambas swam within his eye sockets. The third of that unholy trinity had burrowed through his chin, its nose replaced with that of their host.

"Areet, this ought to make him reconsider," hoped Piper, hurling a cinder block scrap at him.

The thrown stone connected with what remained

of the snake charmer's face, but had no effect. He stayed on track, now close enough for them to hear his croaky grunts. The red moon tracked him, its intense glare lighting the distant background.

"Crap, it didn't work," Julien reviewed, pulling Blair onto her feet. "We're not fighting him unless there's no other reasonable option. Stick to the original plan: run until we're out of the city center."

They resumed running. The chilly night's wind dried the sweat of their brows as they rounded the corner, passing clock towers trapped in whirlpools.

"Coming up on a dead-end. What's the move?" queried Noah, cognizant of the far-stretching ocean ahead.

Peeking over his shoulder, Julien saw that the snake charmer had nearly closed the gap between them. Oddly, he stopped running when they came to the ocean's rim. A fleshy, gray blob soared over the Elehominum, rotating as it landed an inch shy of the water. Klara rose from its mushy folds, spitting a yeasty beam of blue-black saliva at Blair. She ducked and the putrid projectile hit the snake charmer. His skin molted, falling off his skeleton like the meat on a chicken bone in a spicy stew. The mambas that inhabited him shriveled to near-microscopic proportions.

"You lost me my servant; one of you vill take his place!"

Klara's threat went unfulfilled. A wooden oar struck the side of her face, sending her into a rightward tumble. She collided with a disassembled double-decker bus.

The attacker was a khaki-cloaked figure balancing

in an extended, bulky canoe.

"Get in; she'll gather her bearings soon."

The attacker's voice was feminine and British, though not of a discernible origin. Julien opened his mouth to protest, but Piper had already climbed aboard and hugged the mysterious heroine.

"We're safe with her," she said.

Julien had no reason to disbelieve Piper. He followed her lead, and nodded for Blair and Noah to do the same. The three of them sat on planked seats opposite their cheery classmate and the unnamed benefactor.

"Friend of yours?" questioned Noah.

"Nope," Piper answered, laying her head on the woman's shoulder. "She's me mam."

The woman removed her hood, unleashing a headful of unruly champagne-blonde locks. A purple ribbon was braided into her hair, dangling between a pair of cucumber-green eyes. She had skin reminiscent of white chocolate, its only imperfection a patch of eczema that rimmed her chin. She wore radish-shaped earrings, and smelled like the vegetable.

"It's an honor to meet you, Ms. Woolgar," Julien said.

"While I would have preferred to meet my daughter's classmates under different circumstances, I'm glad everyone is in one piece," she began, sitting and rowing. "Please don't trouble yourselves with these formal titles. We're equals. Ellis will do just fine."

The canoe's previously crouched first mate straightened in the front seat, manning the larger oars. The strenuous, yet continual, movement speedily ferried them from land. Klara, hollering profanities, waddled to the oceanfront. She readied her arms for a dive, but recoiled when clouds crowded the red moon.

"You've got to be kidding me. What kind of supervillain is scared of water?" Julien insulted, rowing.

"I doubt it was a fear of swimming. Probably has something to do with that moon being blocked," theorized Ellis. "Regardless of what the case may be, me and my partner will get you safely to school."

"Gonna spill the tea on ya lil' mute helper?" asked Blair.

"All in due time," Ellis said. "It's best I focus on not slowing our progress with chit-chatter. Me and my partner both pull our own weight on this boat. Equals, you know."

Noah helped row, desperate to be of service. "Don't be so modest; you're a legend. Ten years an Elehominum, and never once knocked doon in a rumble. All-time record for Edenshire's unisex squat, too. Our textbooks say it was 525 kilograms, but I heard the weight was triple that. Either way, it's insane how easily yi'd crush a baddie's head between your legs."

"You must be the Satterly boy," Ellis assumed. "Piper told me you are a prankster. Think disobeying rules is funny, do you? You'll be holding the all-time record for detentions at Edenshire if you don't shape up."

Noah's fanatic smile turned into a frown of dejection. "I…"

"Hold your head high. Piper also tells me you've got a brilliant mind, and a resilient heart. She suspects you'll be a junior professor at the school one day," Ellis said.

"She's a constant headache, but my best friend," chortled Noah, high-fiving Piper.

"Good. Now that the pleasantries are done, can someone explain to me why my daughter is bald?" Ellis requested.

Julien recapped the events that preceded her arrival. The grueling battles with the Oath Keepers and the terrors of their Noyeur Atlantis stint were described in graphic detail. He made sure to highlight Piper's bravery in each instance. By the time the story climaxed, they were ten feet from the almost-barren coastline of Cumberchester Heights. A mud-splattered tract of condemned properties awaited.

"Then you came along to spoil Klara's plans, which reminds me," Julien said, turning to Noah. "How did you figure it was her?"

"When she took her glove off, I saw that she had the same birthmark as Navi'el. I'd recognize that half-moon anywhere."

"I didn't notice it. Should've been more attentive," Julien twined, rowing harder.

"Don't be so hard on yourself, you can't see everything. There were a lot of small factors that tipped me off because of my studies," placated Noah. "Remember what I said about the Serpentine Sect during my test at Chillingham Forest? The Germanic accent and her Persian errand boy were dead giveaways."

"I ain't tryin' to get outta pocket but, it seems everyone's gettin' answers except me. I want the name of this other person," Blair grouched.

"Sure me mam will tell yi. Probably was just wanting us to have something better to chat about on the way back to school," said Piper. "Yi are coming with us, aye?"

Ellis fidgeted with the handlebar of an oar. "I am not. Without my grace, I'm hardly a challenge for Navi'el and his Oath Keepers. This is not my fight anymore."

"Doesn't matter. I'd feel heaps better if yi came," Piper whined.

"My glory days as a Geodactyl were long ago. I'd be a liability," vented Ellis, patting her daughter's hand. "This class has everything it needs to win: a capable leader, a fierce enforcer, and loyal soldiery. What makes you all special is that each of you could fit any of those roles."

"I can't act like having you wouldn't be a big help. Somebody has to guide us, and our envoys are gone," Julien said.

"We'd be unstoppable," pandered Noah. "Yi were the Sergeant at Arms for your class. Strategies and countermeasures come naturally to yi. Do us a solid, and tag along. We could use some pointers."

Docking their boat, the first mate deboarded and inspected the premises. Trashcans were upturned and emptied. Whiskered bats had the misfortune of being shooed away from the dilapidated shack where they perched. The trunks of wrecked, doorless cars were thoroughly searched. Stray cats fled as cigarette cartons and ashtrays littered the ground.

"You young men flatter me. It's wonderful to be so known for my service to the Celortus. Still my answer is no," Ellis abjured. "But there is someone who is willing to take on the job."

The first mate peeled back their hood, voluminous chestnut strands jutting out. Her hairline was defaced with third-degree burns.

"Remain wary of the pursuits of men. Their wills are weak, minds young. Were it not for fear, death would go unlamented. Such is the will of the Celortus for their graced children. Let us pray, let us hope…to partake in communion."

Sister Agnieszka had survived.

CHAPTER VI

Sister Agnieszka gazed at the far-flung red moon. The clouds that smothered it dispersed, allowing that infernal fluorescence to spiral and ignite segments of the water. Underneath the canoe was a graveyard of hydraulic machinery. Cogwheels and gears surrounded an observation post. Two drowned sailors were tied to its kinked window bars by hefty shipboard cables.

The Elehominum embraced their envoy with a group hug. Her tired, gray eyes swelled with tears, yet she did not speak. Instead, she held each of them individually and listened to their throbbing heartbeats. Blair tensed as Sister Agnieszka's stomach pressed against her own, a slight roundness now accentuating it.

"Thought you'd been taken prisoner or worse," Julien said. "Don't go missing on us like that ever again. We've already lost Father Nigel and Ava. Any more deaths of our envoys and I'm liable to become depressed."

"Luckily, I found her before anyone else did," accorded Ellis.

"Me mam, the rescuer," Piper beamed.

"I'm buzzing to know how this happened," said Noah, rubbing his hands together as if preparing for a feast. "I always did dream of being privy to undocumented missions."

"I'll let her tell the story," Ellis delegated.

Sister Agnieszka kneeled, returning a manta ray that washed ashore to the flood. "Once the Leviathan's tail hit me, the breath left my chest. I flew, gasping and slobbering. Our schoolhouse, the fights...everything became a blur. I landed in a bay during high tide. I couldn't keep my head above water, so the waves took me under. When I came up for what I was sure would be the last time, I saw a boat. Ellis saved my life."

"Saw her while I was fishing for my dinner in Gateshead," said Ellis. "Was tough getting past the currents, but I got to her. Took her home and warmed her up with a couple sheets. She told me everything over a bowl of pollock stew. You children are fast learners."

"S'why yi should come. Sister Agnieszka might not've made it if yi weren't there, mam. That proves how great yi are, even without the grace," Piper sermonized, taking her mother's hand.

Ellis kissed Piper's knuckle. "It's time for you to prove how great you are, to yourself. You are smart and courageous. The Celortus could not have chosen a more capable person than my baby to be the next Geodactyl."

Piper let go of her mother's hand, begrudgingly accepting the finality of her decision.

"I don't want to overstep my boundaries or get in your business, but I have to ask, Ms. Woolgar: if you aren't coming with us, what are you going to do?" questioned Julien.

"You're a well-mannered young man, but apparently hard of hearing. I've already told you not to call me that; it makes me feel old," Ellis laughed, utilizing an oar to push her canoe back. "I'll be doing the rounds, searching for anybody who needs help. Thank the Lord for my nursing degree."

"Please be safe, mam. Call the school when yi can," said Piper.

Ellis rowed in reverse, eventually turning the canoe around. "I will. Now go show Navi'el the apple doesn't fall too far from the tree."

Piper smiled and waved until her mother was but a speck on the farthest of reddened water.

"Your mam's name still rings bells. She was special. It has to suck measuring yourself against her, but your potential is on a whole 'nother level," Noah ensured, placing his hand on her shoulder. "Yi come from great stock. You're a future legend, no doubt about it."

"Straight facts, no cap," concurred Blair.

"Wouldn't surprise me one bit if you surpassed your mom. I said it in Noyeur Atlantis, and I'll say it again: you're the bravest, toughest little girl I've ever met," complimented Julien.

"Although you may doubt yourself, I feel it in my bones. You are your mother's child. Her talent runs through your veins," Sister Agnieszka exalted, bowing to Piper. "I realize my past failures reflect poorly on my abilities, but the pep talk Ellis gave me livened my spirit. Allow me the privilege of being your envoy once more, and I can swear that you will earn your place in the Elehominum history books."

Piper touched the nun's burns. "Yi never stopped being our envoy."

"We've all had personal failures. Regardless of the past, no one wants to demote you," assented Julien. "Father Nigel would've given you another chance, and so will we."

"His memory lives on through you," Noah said.

"I am forever thankful for your generosity, but I must be upfront: my bracelet was lost during the struggle to stay afloat," disclosed Sister Agnieszka. "It is a necessity for every envoy because it provides a direct line of communication with the Celortus."

"I've got the next best thing."

Reaching into the back pocket of his jumpsuit, Julien procured a replacement bracelet and slipped it onto Sister Agnieszka's wrist. The straw string tightened independently of his control, and the cubic zirconia wolf head charm vibrated.

"Is that Ava's?" asked Piper.

"Was, yeah," Julien validated. "She gave me it before she died. Her last wish was that I find it a good home."

"Ava dos Anjos. It's a rite of passage for every woman who becomes an envoy to hear her brave tale," said Sister Agnieszka, restarting their travel with hasty steps forward. "I will personally recite it to the woman who succeeds me."

They traversed blocks of weed-covered cottages and overgrown lawns. Flaky water flooded a foreclosed home, pedaling filthy baby carriages and unwashed breast pumps into the tarred street.

"Me and Ava had some words. We ended on a good note, though. I'll dedicate my next kill to her,"

Blair forecasted, stepping over a soiled pamper.

Julien considered suggesting that she take it easy, but given her short temper, chose to engage the nun. "What are the odds Navi'el's set up traps in Edenshire, Sister Agnieszka?"

"Unlikely," downplayed Noah. "The Celortus put enchantments on the schoolgrounds. The uninvited can only come while they're recharging their essences. If my notes are correct, that takes between 4-6 hours on average. It was dumb luck that Victoria and those goons showed up when they did."

"He wasn't asking yi, and did yi forget that the Oath Keepers killed Rabbi Tov and Abigail in his dorm? Had to be more than luck," Piper said, elbowing him.

Noah massaged his arm. "Oh, right. I didn't account for their deaths. Still could be luck."

"It's impossible to predict how long the recharging process is," amended Sister Agnieszka. "Certain lunar and solar positions directly influence the security of the enchantments. I do not know the specifics, but there is literature in the Library of Solstice. Father Nigel wrote a chapter himself."

Beholding the garnet satellite, Julien descried the dark outline of a serpentine body drawn in its central crater. The tail rattled and the head spun 360 degrees. He stopped walking, certain that the moon had moved closer. Then came the whispering menace of Klara's voice.

"I am coming, and my visit vill not be kind."

"She's here," Julien alerted. "How the frick did we let her get so close?"

The panic in his tone stopped the others. Blair, Noah, and Piper surveilled the street's outlying perimeters, their eyes scanning rooftops and front yards alike.

Sister Agnieszka reached into her cloak and debuted a new weapon: nunchucks made of sharpened bones. Blue crosses were imprinted on the chain's links. She twirled it threateningly, demanding that the unseen enemy show themselves.

"What are you on about? Nobody's outside," said Noah.

"Get real. I couldn't have been the only one who heard it," Julien wrangled. "Klara was talking, sounded like she was literally beside me."

"I didn't hear nothin'," disagreed Piper.

"Me neither," Blair said.

A titanium plaque fell from the gable of a brass alehouse, smashing a wine jug. The unexpected racket caused the Elehominum and Sister Agnieszka to assume their fighting stances.

"The Old Chateau," read Julien, analyzing the sign's faded lettering. "Must be the name of this joint. Owner's probably closed up shop for renovations. I don't envy them, spending money on repairing stuff, just to find out the world's in a freaking pandemic."

Noah spied through a cracked window. "Pretty sure the owner knew full well. Yi won't believe who's inside."

Curiosity piqued, Julien joined him in his voyeurism. Pineapple margarita in-hand, Madam Marie one-two stepped along a dancefloor set before a grand stage fitted with poles.

"Lemme see," Piper said, climbing onto Noah's back.

Blair chose the lowermost left-sided pane. "How

about that; she got to Cumberchester Heights faster than we did."

"Unless the Flash is secretly an old Cajun woman, something's fishy," conjectured Julien, raising the bottom sill. "She knows more than she's letting on."

He climbed in and was introduced to the soulful, gruff melodies of a blues singer. Undetected, he watched Madam Marie sway and mumble lyrics that spoke to the travesties of Jim Crow, all the while observing the alehouse's features.

Portraits of cancan dancers decorated the spotty walls. Bowls of whipped cream and chocolate sauce were stationed on the rims of roulette tables. A vinyl record player sat eight inches to the right of the window's inner sill, perched on a rotatable minibar.

The stage captivated Julien most. Gummy bears, sour apple lollipops, and jelly beans cluttered the apron. Crotchless thongs were tied on the poles. Raspberry-tinted lights animated an electronic board suspended from the vaulted ceiling, confirming the establishment's name.

"Hold your horses, Piper, we both can't fit in at once," Noah said.

Julien turned to quiet his classmates, but it was he who Madam Marie caught. Wrapping one arm around his neck and the other around his waist, she guided him across the floor's laminate tiles in spins.

"I want to ask you some more questions."

"Later for the jaw-jackin', love. Show me you can groove like Jean-Renee. Your great-grandpappy had genuine rhythm in his hips. He could dance bachata better than the Dominicans."

The record switched to a tune invigorated by

tenor-sung Spanish lyrics and quick guitar strums.

Breaking their hug, Madam Marie held Julien's hand as she coasted back and forth in a three-step motion. She lifted his arm and swiveled, a growing tear showcasing the plumpness of her left buttock.

Infatuated with Madam Marie's jiggly backside, Julien spoke haltingly as it grazed his pelvis.

"Ahem, um, so...h-how did you leave Lacroque so quickly?"

"Sure that's what you really wanna ask, suga? Young bucks got a lot more to be curious 'bout, and ain't no betta teacher than a Cajun mama."

Blair broke the record player's stylus, silencing the music.

"Excuse me, but my ward is 15-years-old and has more pressing matters to tend to than what you want to 'teach' him," declared Sister Agnieszka. "I'm told you were fond of his great-grandfather. Do not confuse the two."

Humming, Piper surveyed the candy selection. "Maybe they look alike, or she could be senile."

"Lordy, how embarrassing," Madam Marie moaned, releasing Julien's hand. "Must've been the alcohol playing jokes on my mind. For a hot minute, I swear I saw Jean-Renee in this boy. I just wanted to boogie with him one last time. Didn't mean no harm."

"Stevie Wonder could see you had some 'dirty dancing' on ya mind, but that ain't even important right now; there's a bigger picture. What I wanna know is: how did ya know exactly when to leave ya lil' rinky-dink pub?" interrogated Blair.

"What are you implying, girly?" Madam Marie rebuffed.

"I ain't implyin' nothin', I'm sayin' it outright: it's real shady that you somehow got outta dodge before we were chased by a half-snake maniac," accused Blair.

"Way too odd to be a coincidence, if yi ask me," Noah said, locking the front door.

Julien shut the window. "I didn't meet my great-grandfather while he was alive, but I'm sure he would've wanted you to tell the truth. You say you loved him, and that you saw him in me, right? Well, think of how badly hurt he'd be knowing that you're purposely lying to his family."

"I saw the red moon hang low. Made me think of the evening she murdered my daddy," whimpered Madam Marie, gulping the remainder of her drink. "One of the last things Jean-Renee taught me was how to get from one place to another in a jiffy. It's easy to screw the process up and lose a limb, so he had me promise to use it only if I was in immediate danger. I'm not too proud to admit I was terrified."

"Could be useful to us. How's it work?" Noah questioned.

"You cut yourself and use your blood to draw a compass on the ground. Then you step on it, and lean toward the direction your destination's in. Most importantly, you gotta be able to clearly visualize where you wanna be," educated Madam Marie. "Jean-Renee would always say you could make lines and curves to point out directions that lead through the walls of space to other spaces beyond, but if you can't concentrate, your brain will fry itself trying to make sense of everything. See, the mind bends and twists to deal with the horrors of life. Sometimes, it bends so much that it snaps in two."

Piper dropped a lollipop in horror. "Sounds awful."

"I forbid it. My wards will not risk handicapping themselves for an escape that may not be viable," Sister Agnieszka ruled.

"Sista, he asked, I told him. Simple as that. I ain't fixing to sway nobody's choices," capitulated Madam Marie.

"Can't argue with her there," Julien justified. "She's cooperating, so why don't we ease up a little?"

"In the mood for answerin' questions, huh? Snitch on who this 'she' is that murked ya pops then," said Blair, pointing the stylus at Madam Marie.

"Didn't care to learn the hussy's name 'cus what she did alone was enough for me to remember her forever," Madam Marie testified. "Daddy owned Newcastle's first textile sweatshop. He had those Africans working their fingers to the bone, but wasn't gonna let no harm come to 'em. When this strange-looking lady randomly showed up needing workers for some private party, he got bad vibes."

"Everything must have gone south from there," said Julien.

Madam Marie bit a pineapple chunk. "They were arguing and then the sky outside went red. I was so busy looking out the window that I didn't notice the workers running away. By the time I looked at daddy to tell him the moon looked like it was on fire, she was covering herself in this juice. Next thing I knew, she had halfway turned into a snake, and spat in his face. Daddy's head melted clean off."

"A most tragic ending for your father," Sister Agnieszka sympathized. "How did you avoid the same fate?"

Frowning, Blair crossed her arms. "Yeah, inquirin' minds wanna know."

"Heavens to Betsy, she was doing her damnedest. Ran me all the way back to Lacroque. Wasn't nuffin' but an act of God that Jean-Renee happened to be waiting for me. He pulled out that amulet, said some gibberish, and it sucked her right on in," hearkened Madam Marie.

"And I'm guessing the same spell that kept Lacroque safe is what's keeping this place's electricity running," Julien posited.

"He guards me, even past those pearly gates," said Madam Marie, stumbling to the minibar. "Plus, the Old Chateau is where he had his last sip of the sauce. It'd be a crime to not protect it. Think I'll pour me a tequila on the rocks in his honor."

Upon her fingers gripping a conical bottle's cork top, the lights flickered and went out. The record player rattled, its squared cartridge discharging dim sparks. Then something heavy and slimy shot through the window, and briskly streamed across the floor.

"Telling family stories, are ve? You mustn't forget zee best part. Tell zem vat sounds your papa made as his skin bubbled. It vas like a frog, no?"

The red moon's profane brightness illuminated the alehouse, revealing that the blob form of Klara was behind Madam Marie. Arising from the ashen mush, she took her by the hair. Drunkenly wiggling, the old woman labored to free herself but failed.

"This hag's relentless," Noah jeered.

"Like those pesky flies who spoil family picnics," said Piper.

"Let's see how she fancies this," Blair bid, tossing the record at Klara.

The disc was hacked with a mere swipe of her tail. "I vould advise you not to try zat again. I could get antsy, and accidentally break zis fragile voman's neck."

"Don't worry; I'll land every hit," Sister Agnieszka said, whirling her nunchucks.

Julien touched the nun's wrist. "No, it's pointless fighting her; she can't be killed. If we're going to save Marie, we'll have to do what she says."

"Come bow at my feet," Klara stipulated. "Perhaps ve can strike a deal."

"She's a lowdown liar, don't y'all trust a word she says," counteracted Madam Marie, reinitiating her futile struggles.

Julien kneeled and directed everyone else to do the same. Noah and Piper unequivocally accepted his command. Sister Agnieszka was much slower to take a knee, her shaky hands squeezing the handles of her weapon. Blair did not move a muscle.

"Are you deaf, or do I need to come break your ickle ankles," an angry Klara offered, jerking Madam Marie's head to the left.

"Nobody orders me on my knees," shunned Blair. "And I'd like to see ya try to break anything of mine. You must not know who I am, but keep chattin' tough and you'll find out I get busy."

"Zee Celortus were quite liberal in picking you. Zey vere not always fond of foulmouthed hoodlums."

"And what about your homies? Were the pickings slim, or do they always go for triflin', horse-faced bimbos with bad boob jobs? I'm sensin' a theme."

Capitalizing on their quarrel, Julien fished the

amulet out of his pocket and outstretched his arm.

"Someone needs another timeout," he exulted, pushing it toward Klara to add emphasis to his statement.

Concern grew as the six-pointed star did little more than pulsate in Julien's hand.

Sneering, Klara swatted the Elehominum and their envoy with her tail. They were sent tumbling to the foot of the stage. Blair had the fortune of landing on top of Sister Agnieszka, whereas the others slammed into a wooden barricade.

"What gives? You should be back inside the amulet," Julien said, massaging his rib.

"Aww, is your toy defective?" gibed Klara. "Mine isn't. You remember how it verks, yes?"

Pinching Madam Marie's nostrils shut, the ghoulish enchantress forced her mouth open and spat a blue-black spitball into it. Choking, Madam Marie fell to the floor and literally coughed up her tonsils. She flailed helplessly as the skin on her face rotted. Within seconds, her eyes, nose, and lips were clumped together in one soupy serving of flesh.

Crawling from under Blair, Sister Agnieszka stood and widened her stance. "Your prey has been taken care of. Therefore, your business here is finished. What more do you want, vermin?"

Klara's bloodlust was unsatiated. She circled Madam Marie's body, drooling on every inch. The smoldered woman's clothes dissolved. A lustrous indigo ring slipped through the ruined seams of her tweed bustier, and rolled to the vamp of Piper's right shoe.

"Why's this piece of crap not working?" Julien

fretted, smacking the amulet.

Dazed, Noah slinked to his side. "Hey, the back has inscriptions on it."

Hearing the revelation, Klara wiped her mouth and resumed blob form. She bounced twice and catapulted out of the fractured window. The red moon's brilliance retreated with her, leaving only the glittery ring to light the Old Chateau.

CHAPTER VII

The Old Chateau's nameboard fell, layering the stage in a bundle of flames and electricity. Liquor bottles burst. Roulette tables were suctioned to the ceiling. They spun fiercely, supplying oxygen to the blooming inferno. Glass shavings darted from the windowsill, skewering Madam Marie's corpse into meaty morsels. A pineapple slice trickled through what was once a colon. Her blood was the dressing to a Cajun salad.

Blown inward at a sideways angle, the front door would have decapitated Julien had he not ducked. Its three jagged hinges speared an oil portrait of twin dancers entertaining a feeble-looking man in a top hat.

"We can't stay here. The protection spells on it are wearing off," Sister Agnieszka regulated, shepherding the Elehominum outside.

Their timing was impeccable. No later than a second after they left the alehouse did a spout of cloudy water uproot it from its understructure. The immense pressure elevated it higher than the other dismal buildings.

Sister Agnieszka and Piper ministered a prayer in remembrance of Madam Marie, proclaiming that God would reunite her and Jean-Renee in the afterlife. The group's observant Catholic twosome left her deathplace, leading the northward pilgrimage.

Hands folded on her stomach, Blair quietly said "amen," did a quick head nod, and followed.

"Marie was doomed from the jump," relented Julien, fingers tracing the amulet's inscriptions. "I don't know how to pronounce these words. Wouldn't surprise me if they were meant for someone with two sets of vocal cords."

Noah took it, and turned it upside down. "They're Old Celortian. Takes some getting used to, but the language really is beautiful. Sounds like a mixture of Hebrew and Swedish when it's spoken. The first eight generations of Elehominum are the only real native speakers, but I'm pretty fluent."

Blair slowed her strides, interested in the boys' conversation.

"Read it aloud."

"Y'sheva baa ra alborg mimi aviv kukutana ha'sadem rosh oüi gakaz kuulin xion naway zalt senai eyþór luo z'undraguv'yig Ålandia tovah."

"Which means what?" inquired Blair.

"I'm iffy on a few words, but the gist of it is saying that this person's blood and essential salts were spilt to forge a personalized prison," Noah translated, returning the amulet to Julien. "Jean-Renee must've had a Grimemory's help in creating this; nobody else knows how to extract essential salts from a living person's body."

Raising her fist, Piper balanced the indigo ring

on the knuckle of her index finger. "And he probably knew an Atlantean. This is pure zaternium."

"How could he have so many connections?" Julien asked.

"We should make haste to Edenshire. While I do not think knowing why your great-grandfather fraternized among certain groups is pertinent to current events, I can respect your desire to research your bloodline," said Sister Agnieszka. "I know very well how the secrets beckon so sweetly. Solomon will guide us to the information."

"That's who Noah mentioned earlier, the timekeeper at the Library of Solstice," Julien recollected.

"Indeed. It is a role he has fulfilled since the school's inception," panegyrized Sister Agnieszka.

"Not much farther now," Noah said. "Just wish the route was more scenic. Cumberchester Heights isn't exactly the prettiest representation of Newcastle."

"Real talk, even my hood is easier on the eyes than this lil' dustheap," censured Blair.

The heart of the seaside village was pure squalor. Delivery wagons were stowed in weedy backyards, winds causing their decrepit wheels to spin eerily. Outhouses, smeared with night soil, polluted the air. Pigpens were plentiful, each serving as a dumping ground for unwanted household appliances.

Businesses and homes that were scorched by the Leviathan's tail blast smoked, cinders of their porches scattering into the floodwater. Blair peered through their windows, yelling that Klara would have to put more effort into her sneak attacks.

Approaching a blackened lodge, Sister Agnieszka

dusted soot off its mailbox. "This is Tyneside Little Angels, the nursery I worked at when I first came from Poland. Father Nigel and I donated soups and coats to them every October. I intend to keep that tradition alive."

"And this was a Greggs. Me mam went to college with two of the cashiers," noted Piper, nodding at a smoldered bakery store beside the nursery.

"That reminds me of something I've been meaning to ask," Julien prefixed. "Why doesn't your mom have a Geordie accent like you and Noah?"

"She's from Evesham, they've got their own twang. It's okay, but I prefer ours," said Piper.

"Props for the clarification, and for this, too," Julien thanked, taking the ring from her and stashing it, along with the amulet, in his pocket. "Might be cool to show it to my dad whenever I go home. His favorite hangout spot as a kid was the Smithsonian National Museum of Natural History."

Noah gulped deeply. "How's he feel about driving in the thick of winter?"

A glacier appeared in the middle of the street, freezing the surrounding water. Long, serrated icicles protruded from its sides. Two girls made their way around the frosted mass, pausing at the front. They both wore the dress variant of Edenshire Academy's uniform, yet were utterly nightmarish.

One girl had a bloated face marbled with black veins, while the other's was scarred by third-degree burns. Their hairstyles were identical: snow-flecked, dark blonde bobs. Earthworms wriggled within the girls' holed ear lobes, acting as macabre jewelry.

"Abigail," Piper muttered.

"And Amelia," said Noah.

"But this cannot be," Sister Agnieszka denied, shaking her head. "I buried them myself."

The undead pair snapped icicles off the glacier, gripping them like swords as the pupils of their brown eyes dilated.

Sauntering, Blair flicked her wrists. "Risen from the dead and beggin' for the whoopin' of a lifetime."

"Na, this is our score to settle. They were our classmates," snubbed Noah, flinging his arm out to stop her progression.

Crouching, Piper picked up a shale and crushed it in one hand. She daubed the rocky residuum across her forehead and then, with her pinky, drew a circle around her bald cranium.

"I trust you two realize that, if you cannot hold your own, Mr. Preux, Ms. Bisping, and myself will intervene. Surely that is fair," Sister Agnieszka bargained.

"It's more than fair," stamped Julien. "We get that this fight's personal, but we aren't rolling the dice with your lives just because you guys have a soft spot for these two. If it so much as looks like you're in over your heads, we're jumping in."

Piper canted her head toward Abigail and Amelia, giving Noah a voiceless signal for a war march. Power-walking, they confronted their former allies.

Julien's flashlight flickered.

"Huh, must need to change these batteries," he said, unscrewing the tail cap.

Suddenly, an orange portal tore open and out of the swirls sprang a saber-fanged black panther with solid white eyes. Latching onto the chain of Sister

Agnieszka's nunchucks, it wrestled the weapon from her hand and dashed behind the Greggs. She gave chase, barking Polish at the unearthly animal.

Julien's attempt to assist in the apprehension was thwarted when Navi'el seized him by the collar of his jumpsuit and slapped the flashlight out of his hand. The High Chief's toffee-colored skin gleamed under the light of new stars, emphasizing the chiseled muscular definition in his bare chest and arms, and his grayscaled half-moon birthmark.

"Was wonderin' when ya would come outta hidin'!"

Following her mouthy assertion, Blair received a swift kick in the chest for trying to free Julien. Reeling, she barreled into a clump of wet trash bags that contained gardening tools.

Navi'el's emotionless saffron eyes averted from her to Julien, the crinkly bangs of his mohawk fluttering in the breeze. He tapped a bloodstain on his deerskin shorts, and dabbed along Julien's throat.

"Those who foolishly travel the jungle are destined to be the apex predator's food."

Lifting his arm, Navi'el conjured a manila rope. It lassoed Julien's neck, lynching him.

"You should have expected me. Your lack of attentiveness will cost you dearly," Navi'el foretold, backsliding into the portal.

Rising sluggishly, Blair grabbed a pair of hedge clippers and staggered to Julien. He was desperately pulling at the binding that constricted his breath, expending precious amounts of oxygen. Gushes of saliva had lubricated the corners of his mouth.

"A hit-and-run? That was a hoe move," said Blair, cutting him down. "I hope ya can breathe easier now, cuz CPR definitely ain't in my wheelhouse."

Julien plummeted to his knees, wheezing and salivating. "We gotta get to Piper and Noah; Navi'el might still be lurking."

"Finally, an executive order I dig," Blair applauded, pulling him up and removing the remaining rope from his neck.

The older Elehominum ran, slipping and sliding their way to combat. There was but a foot of space separating Noah and Piper from Abigail and Amelia. Strangely, neither of the parties had come to blows.

"Nobody's moving. They could be bewitched," said Julien. "Don't worry, guys, we're here!"

Noah turned and blew them onto their backs with a gust of ectoplasm.

"What the hell's your problem?" a furious Blair questioned, hedge clippers skating out of her grasp.

"I told yi already: this is our score to settle, not yours," Noah policed. "They're different from Navi'el's stooges. We won't have yi mutilating our mates."

Julien sat up. "These aren't the people you remember, bro. Let us help."

"Sorry, but Noah's reet; we've gotta do this one on our own," mitigated Piper.

Three-dimensional walls of ice rose around and over Julien and Blair, imprisoning them. Rows of frozen road spikes on the snowy angles and top eliminated their chances of escape. A cranny in a cross-section afforded them a courtside view of the altercation.

"So honorable of you to want a fair fight," Abigail cackled, her cold breaths visible.

"It's the least they could do, dear sister. The debt

they owe for letting us die is steep," upbraided Amelia.

"We barely knew how to use our graces when you were attacked; it wasn't our fault," Noah protested.

Abigail lunged at him with her icicle. "You're a liar!"

"I swear, we'd change history if we could," said Noah, sidestepping and tripping her. "Please don't make us do this. It was tough enough dealing with your deaths."

Piper cautiously reached for Amelia's icicle. "Yi should be resting peacefully, sound asleep in heaven. This wasn't God's plan for yi."

"The Catholic scriptures we were taught are rubbish; he does not exist," Amelia blasphemed, kicking Piper away. "The sky and the cosmos are one. There is only Navi'el. He is the alpha and omega."

Abigail rose onto her knees, stabbing the tip of her blade into Noah's hip and churning.

"We can't let them take on those chicks alone," moderated Julien, banging on the prism's walls.

Blair joined him in the ruckus, but both ceased upon realizing that the activity had caused their hands to become frostbitten. They would have to watch with no way of influencing the fight's outcome.

Purposefully swinging her icicle, Amelia sought to behead Piper. Piper sprawled and Amelia stumbled over Abigail, giving Noah the opportunity to punch her square on the nose. He wrenched the glassy tip from his hip and, in tandem with Piper, bowled toward the glacier.

"Boy, they better have something clever in mind getting so close to that thing," Julien worried. "Wouldn't surprise me if it shapeshifted into the fricking Abominable Snowman."

"Give the yutes a lil' credit; they're smarter than ya think. Got mad guts, too, bruv," said Blair.

Noah broke off two icicles and passed one to Piper. "If this is how it's gan be then so be it. Guess it's time for some tough love."

"Forgive us for what we're about to do," Piper sniffled, polishing the base of her weapon. "I never wanted this for either of yi. I'm so sorry."

The two teams ran at each other. Ice chippings flew as they dueled, swiping hard and fast.

"Where was this wanton courage when Magdalene burned me alive?" reviled Abigail, driving her knee into Noah's stomach.

Noah was momentarily stunned, but recovered with an upward slash. "Had it all along. You dying made me want to be stronger."

Despite blocking his counter, the brunt of it wobbled Abigail. Her shoulder banged against Amelia, who was dead-locked in a contest of fencing with Piper.

"Don't think Noah meant to do that, but I sure am glad he did," Julien said.

"Wish they'd butcher these creeps," spectated Blair. "Old friend or not, I ain't gonna spare nobody who's lookin' to poke me up. Them two would be dogfood."

A husky roar came from the direction in which Sister Agnieszka had run, overtaking Blair's focus.

"I wouldn't wanna raise your expectations, but your wish might get granted," Julien gambled, redirecting her attention to the action.

Plunging his icicle downward, Noah nailed Abigail's foot to the sleet. Rather than holler in agony, she cut him across his bottom lip, adding to the self-inflicted scars that simulated an everlasting smile on his face. Screaming, he lurched backward, yanking the icicle out of her gushing wound.

Unaffected by the wails, Piper parried two of Amelia's slash attempts and tripped her.

Abigail thrashed Noah with a punch to the back of his head, and set her sights on Piper.

"Surprise, surprise. The littler Geordie *is* a fighter, unlike the pasty-faced boy. Why don't you consider shedding the dead weight?"

"You're wrong; Noah's a fighter through and through. Our town's known for 'em."

"Come, show me that Newcastle upon Tyne is where the brave of heart dwell!"

Welcoming the challenge, Piper lunged but was intercepted at the ankle by Amelia's decayed hand.

"Oh, how willingly you've wandered into our trap."

Julien and Blair instinctively grabbed one another's hand as they watched what could be the death sequence for their youngest classmate.

"Indeed, sissy. She always was a headstrong goody two-shoes," Abigail sneered, raising her icicle in preparation to stake Piper. "Shall we see how she does without a head at all?"

"Sorry, I don't much fancy headless friends," said a recuperated Noah, cinching the murderous zombie in a one-armed stranglehold.

Julien clapped. "Awesome torque on that sleeper. If he cranks up the tightness, Abigail won't have any choice but to faint."

"She's already dead. Breathin' probably doesn't affect her how it would somebody that's alive," Blair commentated. "I've seen this trick a million times; she's fakin'. Watch her body movements."

Bending at the knees, Abigail clenched Noah's forearm and flipped him over her shoulder. He landed on his feet, trampling Amelia's wrist and disengaging the grip she had on Piper.

"Cheers, I was looking for more creative ways to get my daily exercise done. Gotta sculpt the ol' six pack."

Noah's sarcasm frenzied Abigail. Snarling, she chased him toward the glacier. He ran up a series of icicles and backflipped, repositioning himself at her rear. With a heavy-handed shove, he impaled her on the sheeny, barbed ends.

"You and him are merely prolonging your deserved punishments," Amelia browbeat, rising with a swing at Piper. "It was your ineptitude that cost us our lives. We will avenge ourselves."

Piper ducked, circled Amelia, and connected with a dropkick that propelled her face-first toward the glacier, where she was ultimately impaled beside Abigail.

"Thank goodness we've put those nightmares to bed," said Noah, casting his icicle aside. "They weren't themselves. Neither of them would ever say that sort of stuff."

Piper did the same with hers. "Didn't enjoy it, but it had to be done."

The Geordies shook hands, complimenting each other's bravery. Their praises soon suffocated under resounding snickers. Abigail and Amelia jerked their bodies off the prongs, shivering as their wounds closed.

"This is bad," Julien deduced. "Who the heck laughs after they've been given body piercings that big?"

"Psychos who've got nothin' to lose," Blair responded.

The glacier ejected its surviving icicles, instantaneously freezing buildings and stray animals. Grinding itself against the pavement, it took the shape of a crystalline wolf's paw.

"Enough child's play," Abigail guffawed, spitting out a tooth. "Shall we show these two we are still Elehominum?"

Amelia loosened her collar. "I thought you'd never ask, dear sister."

Pale gray and sky-blue sparkles coursed through the paw's nails, triggering twitches.

CHAPTER VIII

Abigail and Amelia clawed away the defiled skin that made up their lips and cheeks. Shreds of tissue sagged to their receding chins, pouring maggot eggs onto the sisters' dress straps. The pests hatched and wiggled under the buttons, suspicious of the trembles that followed their birth. Piper and Noah grimaced as their former classmates wrenched at their jaw bones. The dental demolition produced noises akin to slow glass shatters.

"Christ, what now?" Julien dreaded.

"Prolly something straight outta a Quentin Tarantino movie," predicted Blair.

The subzero sisters removed their jaw bones, exposing the black ice molds of their mouths hidden behind them. Teeth glittering, they sprayed beams of white slush at Noah and Piper. Both Geordies evaded the blasts, but were unsteady on the slippery sleet.

Julien's eyes enlarged with astonishment. "They weren't bluffing about still being Elehominum."

"And they're mad dangerous when they're together," Blair said. "Amelia's an Icevous, which is somebody graced by hail. Abigail's a Glaciacht, so she's graced by snow. Father Nigel gave me the lowdown on 'em while we were preparin' my lecture. They can freeze a person's bloodstream in a couple of minutes."

"This might be harder to watch than I thought," adjudged Julien, biting his nails.

A storm of leaden pellets pelted Piper, burying the Geodactyl up to her neck. Noah pawed at the arctic encasement, laboring to dig her out. He had just about freed her when a succession of snowflakes pounded his rotator cuffs and lower spine. The impacts sent him side-winding across the ice.

Abigail and Amelia leaped ten-feet into the air, frozen in place until Noah's body thudded against a forklift tire. Skydiving, they pounced on his injured hip with stomps.

"Abigail pricking him didn't draw much blood," Julien said. "They're morons if they think an incision that small will cause someone to bleed to death."

"They've got worse plans," forewarned Blair.

Gashing a hole through Noah's left pant leg, the sinister siblings laid their hands on his wound. He screeched as the red specks and bruises on his hip turned glasslike.

"Dead for who knows how long, yet we haven't missed a beat. Our old tricks are unbeatable," Amelia boasted. "Contuse the skin, and the coldness will funnel in."

Abigail raked her fingertips up Noah's inner thigh. "I could not agree more, sissy. He'll be a gorgeous snow angel at the stroke of midnight."

"Nah uh. I ain't gonna stand for this mess. Lil' bro-bro probably already has hypothermia," fumed Blair, pounding on the impenetrable enclosure's frigid walls.

Julien triumphantly upraised his arm. "Don't go abandoning hope too fast; we've still got our ace. She's 50 pounds of dynamite."

Shimmying madly, Piper had managed to disentangle herself. She headbutted the ground and onset a tremor. The unexpected quake threw Abigail and Amelia onto a moth-eaten porch.

"Ey, that's what I wanna see," Blair celebrated. "She's boutta get it crackin'. Tweedledee and Tweedledum will be sorry they ever touched Noah. On Father Nigel nem grave, it's merched."

"Those two argue nonstop, but they do *not* play about each other," said Julien.

Piper slid to Noah and checked his pulse.

"Now I know what it feels like to be a pint of Ben & Jerry's Chunky Monkey," he wisecracked.

"I told yi to stop eating that so often; it makes you fart," prescribed Piper. "Here's the consequences for not listening to me."

Noah yelped as she peeled off his icy scabs.

"Good grief, woman! Are you an Elehominum, or one of the Queen's executioners?"

"Quit your blabbering, couldn't have been worse than removing a bandage," Piper undermined, grinning.

The wolf paw spasmed and, as if they were controlled by puppeteer strings, Abigail and Amelia were whisked onto their feet.

"That glacier's empowering them. We need to destroy it," incentivized Noah.

"It'll be hard with them trying to kill us," Piper said. "But we'd better do something fast. They're moving."

Firmly grasping ejected icicles, Abigail and Amelia swallowed them whole and sputtered the glazed slivers like nail guns.

Piper rapped on her forehead and gripped a segment of the ground that was defrosted by the tremor. Levering it up, she shielded herself and Noah from the projectiles. The erected barrier, composed of dirt clods and gravel, did not budge.

"Good on her for thinking quickly, but they can't use that rock wall for cover forever," Julien analyzed.

"True, cuz Abigail and Amelia ain't no sittin' ducks," said Blair, referencing their return to the battleground. "Piper and Noah gotta be smart. Those ain't their friends no more; they're killers."

Julien squinted. "I see their lips moving. I'd love to know what they're saying, but my guess is they're purposely keeping their voices low. Element of surprise, maybe?"

Noah whispered something in Piper's ear and edged from behind their blockade. Pursing his lips, he breathed an ectoplasmic wildebeest into existence. The ghostly animal was colored with various blacks. Its curved horns excessively leaked purple droplets, obscuring what was presumably a face.

Unafraid, Abigail and Amelia skated onto the rink. Their forearms had sprouted ice-encrusted pitchforks.

"I've learned loads since you two have been gone," Noah trumpeted, straddling the wildebeest. "Hex here, hex there. A hex for he and she, why care? A bottomless hex, a bottomless sea, source of all misfortune, all ill things that be. Listen for the sorrowful chants. Weep with them, as one does in trance. And weep with me, yes, weep with me."

He exhaled and dark violet goo armored his body, giving him the appearance of a knight submersed in liquified lavender. Vomiting an enameled katana, the wildebeest delivered it to him with its tongue and plowed ahead.

"Whoa, that is insanely epic. He'd give Hollywood costume designers a run for their money," admired Julien, readying himself to climb for a closer view.

A jolt of frostbite changed his mind.

"Try not to be such a fanboy," Blair carped.

"Dear oh dear, Noah's found some use for his legendary spell book," snickered Amelia, skating a figure eight. "What ever shall we do? We're powerless to stop the big, bad magician."

Abigail performed a one-foot spin. "Right you are, sissy. We should be trembling in our boots, if only we didn't remember the truth: his two-bit illusions barely last a minute."

"Got my fingers crossed that what they mentioned about Noah having a time limit is baloney, but they aren't backing down," Julien distressed.

"They ain't scared," said Blair. "But neither is our phantom boy."

Charging, Noah and his familiar intended to ram the resurrected Elehominum. However, Abigail and Amelia corkscrew somersaulted, rotating 630 degrees as they blew hailstones that manufactured icebound ramps.

"Not exactly my idea of a winter wonderland, and they wouldn't be anyone's first choices for Santa's little helpers," Julien assessed.

"Nope, but their Christmas is about to be spoiled," anticipated Blair.

Noah's wildebeest swung its horns at Abigail and Amelia as they glided along its sides. Ducking, both avoided the attempted stabs.

"Did you really think we would keep pairing off against the two of you?" Amelia heckled. "What would possess you to have such idiotic thoughts?"

"Mischievous little bastard must've forgotten: we fight as one," surmised Abigail.

The living dead sisters swiped for the wildebeest's spindly legs. A fast-hardening gas curbed the prongs of their pitchforks.

"A true Wolven scholar doesn't forget much," Noah said, his voice slightly muffled by that gooey helmet. "Yi haven't got anything I can't handle on me own."

Abigail jabbed her pitchfork at his face. "Time's winding down for your mirages."

Leaning backward, Noah used his sword to chop the horrendous growth in half. She careened off course, crashing into a pile of armless baby dolls.

"The nerve of you, daring to challenge your superiors," blustered Amelia, repeating Abigail's failed action.

After dodging left, Noah thumped her nasal bridge with the handle of his sword. She tottered, but did not cease her pursuit.

Skating to the right of the wildebeest once again, Abigail contoured what was left of her ruptured pitchfork into an asymmetrical arrow. "I'll bet you believed what you did was clever. Well, all you did was give me a new way to hurt you."

Noah did not reply. He spanked the wildebeest's backside and it vaulted into the air.

Coasting up ice ramps, the two former Edenshire

Academy students were unabated. Their mandibles shimmered in the moonlight as they went airborne.

"Time's up," they said, grabbing hold of the wildebeest's knotty mane.

Abigail and Amelia impaled the ethereal creature with their weapons a second before it was due to land atop a barn roof. Dissipating in a puff of plum smoke, it dropped Noah. Skidding across bacon grease and rooster feathers, he found himself face-down under an assembly table. His ectoplasmic armor and sword evaporated.

"Sheesh, I wouldn't have expected that freaky antelope to die so easily," belittled Blair. "What's the use in conjurin' a ghost if it can't take a hit?"

"We've got bigger problems to worry about than the practicalities of ectoplasm," Julien said.

Abigail snatched Noah's head up by his platinum locks. "What deep-rooted troubles these lovely eyes must hold."

"Eyes are the windows to the soul," tittered Amelia, tickling around his eyebrow with her pitchfork. "Let us discover what lies in his."

"Where the hell's Piper?" Blair squawked.

"There," reported Julien.

Piper had been hard at work, molding the rock wall into a boulder. Brown flickers outlined the circumference. Cobble and coal fortified its composition. Begrimed hands steadying it, she gave one mighty push with her forehead. The earthen ball shot for the glacier, instantly shattering it and taking its place in the street.

Abigail and Amelia collapsed. Overturning the table, Noah latched onto their shirt collars and hauled them to the roof's rain gutter. He hugged both to his chest and slid down an ice ramp.

"So that's what they were whispering about," Julien registered. "It was a diversion so Piper could destroy their power source."

"Told ya they're smarter than ya give 'em credit for," said Blair.

The wintry fort that jailed them thawed.

Feeling warmth on his calloused palm, Julien realized he and Blair were still hand in hand.

"I really am sorry for how I treated you at Lacroque, Bee. It was the stupidest thing anyone could ever say."

"You meant those words. I'ma make you eat 'em."

"If I could take it back, I would. I can understand you not forgiving me, I just don't want our differences affecting anybody else. What's between us, is between us."

Letting go of each other's hand, the elder Elehominum stepped over shafts of melted ice. Blair power-walked along the defrosted surface, meeting Noah and Piper at the watery slope where a rimed ramp once stood.

Kneeling to retrieve his flashlight, Julien heard a high-pitched growl and the unmistakable guttural cadence of Sister Agnieszka's voice. Expecting to see her striding victoriously, his head turned left but he saw no such sight. Standing, he hastened to reconvene with his classmates.

Piper crumbled clay soil onto the necks of Abigail and Amelia. Thickening around their temples, the fine-grained earth locked their heads in position to stargaze. Pinching both girls' nose close, Noah set his eyes on the single cloud in the sky.

"Are they alive?" Julien whispered to Blair. "I'm not sure what to make of them just falling all willy-nilly."

"Your guess is as good as mine, genius. I've been here for maybe nine seconds longer than you," she said, shrugging.

Pressing a finger to her lips, Piper motioned for them to stop speaking, and rolled up Noah's sleeves.

"Glory be to the names of my greatest precursors: Sebastian the Sinful, Beatrice the Blasphemous, Isaac the Irreverent," he invoked, royal purple haze seeping through his pores. "Glorious Grimemories of days gone, lend me your sullen strength to unshackle these victims from spiritual bondage."

Abigail and Amelia shuddered and their ears discharged an inky secretion. The puddle in which they floated sizzled as the water and that unidentified substance blended.

"Break these demonic ties, liberate the enslaved," impetrated Noah.

Hollow, sparkly versions of Abigail and Amelia arose from their bodies. Humming fireflies orbited them, spraying misty vapors. Their original mouths were restored, and the grotesque, forearm-centered instruments they wielded were no more.

"Holy cow," Julien marveled.

"Hello," said Abigail and Amelia, bowing.

A tear ran down Piper's cheek. "Please don't have us fight yi again."

"Know that we wouldn't willingly raise our fists to you nor Noah in anger. We were not in control,"

Amelia swore.

"It was like we were just passengers in our own bodies," evoked Abigail. "But we saw and felt everything. You two were brilliant."

Noah wiped away his own tears with the hem of his cape. "The dead don't walk unless someone reanimates them. Do you remember how this happened?"

"We shared the same dream, one where we frolicked in a sunlit field of lilies. It was so warm, and bright," began Amelia. "Then we heard rain. The weather became very cold and windy."

"When our eyes opened, we were strapped to operating tables in a surgery room infested with living plants," Abigail continued.

"Dr. Jung's lab in Noyeur Atlantis," mouthed Julien.

"Men in white coats jammed tubes into our veins, and pumped us full of something glutinous and blacker than oil. Our graces circled our heads, brightly colored in orb form. The last thing we saw before fighting you was Navi'el's face," Amelia said.

"We weren't the only ones he reanimated, either," hinted Abigail. "Rabbi Tov was there. He worked the machine the tubes were hooked up to."

"No, no, this isn't fair," Noah repeated, punching a block of ice.

"We can't hurt our old envoy. This is becoming too much," puled Piper.

Amelia placed her hands over her heart. "He is not himself. You would be doing him a service to end his half-life. A man that great should be rewarded with eternal peace, not an afterlife of slavery."

"Is it possible that we can save him?" Piper wept.

"Dead-riser hexes are notoriously tricky. The older a person is, the harder it is for them to resist the influence that reanimated them," said Noah. "Rabbi Tov had Father Nigel by five years. His chances of remembering how much he cared for us are slim. The envoy honor codes he believed in are likely forgotten."

"Slay him," Abigail persisted, her eyes welling with bioluminescent tears.

"It must be done. You have no alternatives," necessitated Amelia.

"Tell us where he is," Blair instigated.

"Step lightly round to the right of the abandoned distillery, and seek an olden, shrouded synagogue," coordinated Abigail.

"Ner Tamid, it's the Reform temple where Rabbi Tov taught courses on rabbinic law," Noah expounded, sniffling. "On starry June evenings, fog covers the door and balcony. Local legend says it comes from the ghosts of Jews who attended services there. They cling onto it because they're afraid of what might be waiting for them once they've passed on."

Piper paced in a circle, balling and unballing her fists. "Why does it have to be us? No other Elehominum has had to kill their envoy."

"God gives his toughest battles to his strongest soldiers," propagated Amelia.

Noah chewed his lips as more tears streaked his face.

"Graced children, dry these tears that trickle down your cheek," Abigail beseeched. "They are weaknesses leaving your bodies. In times of hardship, it will be your new classmates that strengthen you. You must pull yourselves together to ensure that you can do the same for them when need be. They cannot defeat Navi'el without you."

Julien hooked Noah's arm and pulled him to his feet. "Brothers in arms."

"Warrior women of the west," Blair said, clapping Piper on the back.

"A united home front," federated Amelia.

"We see it. You were meant to find them, to fight alongside them," Abigail blazoned, grinding her knuckles into her palm. "Do not mourn our deaths. Rejoice in knowing that this class is the one to which you truly belong."

"We miss you," bleated Noah.

Amelia smiled, resting a see-through hand on his cheek. "Friends to infinity, and beyond."

"If only heaven had visiting hours," Piper imagined.

"What's it like to die?" asked Noah. "Is there really a God?"

"Arisen dead cannot share explicit eldritch truths with the living; the veil between both planes of existence is blurred by a dream we cannot fully remember when awakened," Abigail imparted.

"The universe has safeguards put in place to curb the activities of madmen who wish to cheat death. It is best to focus on the here and now. Be kindhearted and gentle not because you fear damnation, but because humility separates us from the Mavkardia," inculcated Amelia.

Noah's hazy emissions dissipated.

"Goodbye, dear friends. It was a pleasure hearing your voices again," Abigail and Amelia said, conjoining at the hip.

The girls dipped, reentering their physical bodies.

They burst into an explosion of whiteness, leaving no evidence of their profane resurrection.

Shallow ice cracked under the resurgence of footsteps. Shouldering her nunchucks, Sister Agnieszka advanced toward the group. Her face was newly scarred with claw marks. Kneeling where Abigail and Amelia had been, she clasped her hands together and prayed to the night sky.

"O Celortus, of the elements, of the Earth...oh, fleeting will of the ancients. Let the Drescott twins be safe, let them find comfort, and let the dream, their caretaker, foretell a rapturous awakening. May their service as Elehominum be one day a fond, distant memory."

CHAPTER IX

Sister Agnieszka's facial abrasions had not gone unnoticed. The Elehominum bombarded her with inquiries about her private clash with that monstrous panther, citing concerns of internal organ damage. Their worries intensified when the scratches bled. The ice arch above her sprang a leak, dribbling water that evanesced atop her head. Those chestnut brown hairs curled at the roots, and the ends flattened like makeshift sideburns. Unfazed, she did not respond.

A solitary raindrop splashed into Piper's palm. She delicately brushed at the nun's bloodstains.

"Try not to be too heavy-handed with that water," Julien monitored. "It's probably not the cleanest, and we don't want her getting infections."

Standing up straight, Sister Agnieszka suckled dried blood off her lower lip. "I apologize for scaring everyone. Ten seconds of silence after saying a prayer for the fallen is a sacred tradition of my covenant."

"Thank goodness, because those claw marks are brutal. We weren't sure what to think," said Noah.

"That thing ain't hurt you much, did it," Blair asked.

"I've never skinned an animal, but got no problems doin' that one alive. Wouldn't mind makin' me some snakeskin boots outta Klara's tail, either."

"I am fine, though I can't say the same for Navi'el's pet," insinuated Sister Agnieszka, brandishing an extensive backbone from underneath her cloak.

Noah gawked at the sheer length and girth. "Blimey, that is ginormous. Must've belonged to a lion."

"Whatever this was, it had seventeen thoracic vertebrae," Julien documented, counting the hook-shaped bones. "I'm no veterinarian, but I think that's more than a tiger has. Tigers are generally bigger than lions. Respect to you for killing this hefty boy."

"I'm sure Father Nigel would be proud," hailed Piper.

"I appreciate the praise, but we must be on our way," Sister Agnieszka reiterated, knotting the backbone to the chain that linked her nunchucks. "We're sitting ducks here. Us lollygagging only benefits Navi'el."

Blair cracked her middle fingers. "And we can't forget about that witch Klara neither."

"Sister Agnieszka's right; there aren't any moments for us to spare. Stay alert, everybody," Julien superintended, guiding the collective's warpath.

They maneuvered around the boulder Piper designed, venturing farther into Cumberchester Heights. The floodwaters had tapered off tremendously, barely sloshing when stomped, yet reeked of sulfuric acid. Plastic bags filled with crab shells barricaded the entrance of a grimy woodshed. Roadkill lay on barbecue pits, blow flies buzzing about the grills. Clotheslines hung holey turtlenecks, peacoats, and blouses.

"I always knew da Heights was bad, but this reminds me of a third-world country," said Blair. "I wonder how the people who live here can stomach it."

"Most shack themselves up in their houses and I can't blame them. Society treats old people horribly, and don't even get me started on the mentally unstable. My uncle Jonty is slightly autistic, and welfare services used that to say he was unfit to take care of me after ma and da died. Proppa ruined me faith in humanity, tha' did," Noah griped.

"It's despicable how they're treated," chided Sister Agnieszka. "The least the city council could do is have groceries delivered to them."

"We should knock on everyone's door, and ask if they've got enough food," Piper endorsed.

Julien stopped walking. "I don't know about all of them, but I do see one door in particular we should knock on."

A chrome jet ski was parked on the mossy lawn of a maple cottage. Its engine sang low grumbles.

"That numpty MacGregor isn't the greatest at hiding his location, is he? It's almost like he wants to get caught," Noah scrutinized.

"He can't be this careless," said Julien, spotting the vehicle's keys. "Unless those Commando ranks mean nothing, I have to believe he'd be a little craftier."

"What are you on about? They're suicide bombers at best. Blaxburg was the only one with half a brain," Blair contradicted.

The cottage's door sagged off its hinges, allowing the smells of apple, cinnamon and raisins to waft outside.

"Seems we've caught him in the middle of cooking a meal," figured Sister Agnieszka.

"Guess who's coming to din-din," Noah leered.

Julien took a big step forward. "Nobody, at least not until I scope it out first. Wait for my signal."

Entering, he scanned the dismal abode's layout. The original brown paintjob of the walls had been dirtied with swatted insects and mold. Wheat toast crumbs overspread the squeaky, cork floor. Cod floundered on the ceiling. Two tureens of oatmeal covered a coffee table arrayed in front of a busted television. The doorway that led to a peninsula kitchen was obstructed by a fizzing cascade.

A staircase missing every other step sat left of a fireplace.

Changing his flashlight's battery, Julien shined the light on Blair. He paused, studying the fullness of her belly. A vision of a fast-growing fetus spellbound his mind. Its harrowing cry deafened him.

Piper canted into his line of sight. "Yi didn't tell us what the signal was. Does that mean it's safe to come in?"

"Sorry, got caught up in my thoughts," Julien said, waving his allies inside. "Be light on your feet; the floor looks janky."

Piper, Blair, and Noah trooped in a single-file. Stealing the jet ski's keys, Sister Agnieszka pitched them over the boulder and entered.

"Not much to see down here, but I haven't looked up there yet," stated Julien, aiming the flashlight at the staircase.

"Imagine if we find this bloke, snug in his blankets and eating a bagel. The bastard's britches might boil from how hard he craps himself," Noah relished.

"He'd better savor every bite cuz this'll be his last supper," said Blair.

"Let us not be so quick to kill," Sister Agnieszka weighed, kneading the addition to her nunchucks. "He may be of more use to us alive than dead. Insider information on Navi'el's plans is invaluable."

Tiptoeing to the staircase, Julien gripped the rust-colored banister and ascended. "Be careful going up these stairs. This cottage is in rough shape."

The Edenshire Academy affiliates shadowed his lead. They arrived at a hallway with eroded walls, and thumbtacked to them were black and white photographs of a cross-eyed woman and a gaunt boy clinging to her waist. Three rooms were on the upper floor. Two doors were knobless.

Divvying up tasks, the burglars-turned-investigators sought clues that would confirm if an occupant was present. Piper opened the drawer below a lit candlestand, and sifted through crayon drawings of leprechauns. Sister Agnieszka examined the cable wires that bored into the high corners closest to the staircase. Lowering themselves, Julien and Noah peeked under the sill of the unhampered door.

"Whoever owns this lil' roach motel wouldn't be too happy knowin' they've got a lowlife squatter," Blair weened, tearing down one of the photographs. "Then again, she might not even know which direction to look in."

A shot rang from the door where Julien and Noah spied. It struck the hat rack beside Sister Agnieszka.

"Thought ya'd get an easy kill on me, eh? Well, I've got news for you punks: dyin' isn't on my agenda,"

Commander MacGregor announced, firing two more shots.

Piper tucked herself behind the lampstand. Blair backed against a strip of grainy photographs. Whipping her nunchucks, Sister Agnieszka chopped the bullets into lead scraps.

"You're making things awfully hard on yourself," said Julien. "We just came to talk. This doesn't have to end with someone in a casket."

Commander MacGregor audibly reloaded his Luger. "Talk? I'll pass, fella; I don't chit-chat with the enemy."

"Areet, we tried to play nicely," Noah vindicated, breathing a draft of ectoplasm into the door's keyhole.

"Try your luck playing with this, ya little fu…"

A fit of wheezes and coughs silenced Commander MacGregor's foul-mouthed rhetoric.

"I thickened the air in his lungs; he's scrambling for a hint of oxygen," briefed Noah. "Doesn't last long, but it's effective. It's sort of like a short-term asthma attack."

"Time is of the essence," Julien cued, kicking in the door.

Lit by miniature jack-o'-lanterns that decorated the ceiling fan, the hideout was a far-right madhouse. Clippings from Ireland's nationalistic publications plastered the walls. Gaelic phrases were scribbled onto the floorboards.

The Irishman himself was clawing at blackout window curtains.

Julien and his collaborators stormed the room. A waterbed took up most of the space, two six-packs of Windrush Cola cans at its foot. Noah ransacked the closet, plucking sweatshirts off tubular hangers and feeling inside their pouches. He located four faded prescription papers and a pair of handcuffs. Piper rummaged through a rolltop desk, and found syringes and pill bottles. She read the labels, struggling to pronounce the ingredients. Sister Agnieszka guarded the doorway, neutralizing any attempt at a crafty escape.

Blair pounced on Commander MacGregor, wresting the gun out of his hand.

"Breathe wrong, and I'll cook your brains," she levied, sticking the barrel in his ear.

"Won't do ya no good," sneezed Commander MacGregor. "You're too late to stop the High Chief."

Julien lounged on the waterbed, pushing aside a plate of rye toast and pan-fried coco wheats. "You've got two options: you can either die and stay loyal to your boss, who isn't the least bit worried about your wellbeing, or help us and live to see another day."

"Screw the formalities. Lemme pop this joker right now, bruv," Blair raged.

"You're an overly aggressive loudmouth. Typical Brit," rasped Commander MacGregor.

"Excuse me," Noah and Piper chorused.

Blair pistol-whipped him. "What was ya sayin'?"

"You heard me bang on," reasserted Commander MacGregor, his head bumping against the window's stile. "I'm old enough to remember the stories about how ya forefathers treated the Irish who came to England for better opportunities. They made fun o' our accents, and refused to hire us if it wasn't a gig cleanin' shoes. Bless the lasses; the lot o' 'em became whores. The British tried to make sure we'd never be more than potato pickers. Ireland's dignity was stolen by those money-hungry trolls. My heart bleeds for my people, for my homeland."

Clutching the collar of his jacket, Blair threw him to the floor.

"I wouldn't expect you to have this much sympathy for immigrants getting mistreated in a foreign country," Julien said, nodding at the xenophobic articles. "But if you've got all that so-called 'pride' in Ireland, why would you knowingly side with Navi'el? Don't tell me you think he's going to spare your country if his plan succeeds."

"He kidnapped my mum. Told me he'd give her back to me if I joined his army. I was a man who didn't have a choice," deponed Commander MacGregor.

"You believe we're buyin' that Navi'el went *that* far to get you on his team, even though you're obviously a terrible strategist?" Blair affronted. "Does he want to fail? You didn't even have enough commonsense to hide your jet ski, and shorties on the block have better aim than you do."

Commander MacGregor pointed to a hand-drawn geometric graph tacked between two articles promoting islamophobia. "I'm a diabetic; a soldier's life would've never been one fa' me. Rumblin' wasn't my strong suit, but I had book smarts. Was top o' me class. All my schoolteachers said I was born to be an engineer. When me and my mum moved in here, I did the utility repairs. Didn't spend a day in an auto shop, but I rewired our carburetor. Everything came naturally to me."

"Is that jet ski your design, too?" asked Noah, crumpling the papers.

"It is. I'm sure you saw a couple of my prototypes in Noyeur Atlantis as well," Commander MacGregor bragged. "Every shred of Commando gear you see was made by me. I remember drawing up the blueprints like it was yesterday. The shotguns were the most fun to make."

"And now he gloats about sellin' out humanity," arraigned Blair.

"I'd walk through fire for my mum. She worked hard to support us, scrubbin' bathtubs and vacuumin' carpets," Commander MacGregor proudly rambled. "My father's a deadbeat who ran off and married some ugly Paki floozie ten years younger than him. While he was snoggin' her, my mum was takin' me to doctor appointments and stressin' about payin' for my medicine. Her life is more precious to me than anybody else's. Judge me how you please, I really don't care."

Julien pushed off the rubbery mattress, dipping face-level with the bitter officer. "What if I told you that you could save your mom without screwing over the rest of the world?"

"If she's as nice as she sounds, she wouldn't want you doing bad. She'd tell yi to dee what's right," said Piper.

"You really think there's a chance at beating him," Commander MacGregor pried.

"We don't think we can; we know it," amended Julien.

Stillness overtook the room as Commander MacGregor looked from person to person, surveying their adamant facial expressions. A bead of sweat ran down his chapped lips.

"What do I gotta do?" he questioned.

"Take us to where he is," required Julien. "Tell us everything we should be expecting him to do in a fight."

"It would also behoove you to put a filter on your racism," Sister Agnieszka incorporated.

"Fine, but if you start a squabble with the High Chief, you'd better be able to finish it," premised Commander MacGregor. "I got no qualms about sidin' with him if you lot get massacred."

"Oh, quit your wafflin'," Blair said, lifting him by the curl of his orangey beard.

Noah handcuffed Commander MacGregor's arms behind his back. "These ought to prevent any funny biz. Can't have you betraying us too early now, can we?"

"No, o'course not," Commander MacGregor sarcastically replied.

"It would be in your best interest not to, because I have the tendency of getting very physical when my wards are in danger," Sister Agnieszka cautioned. "Now that I've made myself perfectly clear, I see no merit in spending another second here."

"Alright then, folks, we're set. Next stop: Ner Tamid," commissioned Julien.

Blair shoved Commander MacGregor. "What, got plugs in your ears or something? You heard him. Lead the way, soldier."

The temperature outside had decreased by several degrees. Shooting stars hurtled across the night sky, twinkling among an overlay of black and navy-blue. Puddles splish-splashed as the liberators and their hostage furthered their march on Cumberchester Heights, touring its impoverished communities. Bird droppings vandalized traffic signs. The street's stoplights were faulty, dispensing electrical wires and carriage bolts.

Blair personally escorted Commander MacGregor, one hand on his shoulder and the other holding that Luger an inch from his spine. They navigated a winding road, bypassing playgrounds and school buses that juddered on waterways.

"I couldn't say what's stranger: the random waste we're seeing or the fact that some areas are flooded, but others aren't," Julien distinguished, hopping over a beartrap.

"The High Chief's not done with his whole spell," said Commander MacGregor. "Newcastle will be lost to the waves before sunrise, though, I'll bet you. He's a fast worker. It's remarkable, if you ask me."

Blair smacked the neckline of his pompadour. "Get off his nuts. Nobody asked for your opinion."

Gritting his teeth, Commander MacGregor did not retaliate. He led them to a residential block that was untouched by the flood. The homes were identical: redwood composition, smoky chimneys, and drainage pipes swathed in snakeskin sheddings.

"Klara von Schlange, head of the Serpentine Sect, is hunting my wards. I'm sure that you are privy to the intricacies of her role in Navi'el's debauchery," Sister Agnieszka conjectured.

"I'm not entirely sure, but she's a wild one, that lass. Not even the roughest, nastiest Commandos would dream o' mouthin' off to the High Chief the way she does," arbitrated Commander MacGregor. "Can't blame her, though, can you? It has to be tough being the sole survivor o' your clan. You carry the weight o' your culture on your shoulders."

"You're forgetting that Navi'el is also a Mavkardia," Julien marginalized.

"One plus one equals two. Learn to count, dummy," disparaged Blair.

"They're both Mavkardia, yeah, but belong to different clans," Commander MacGregor disseminated, annoyance evident in his tone. "All o' 'em were born from the darkness imploding. They wandered the planet 'til eventually shackin' up in what became the Appalachian Mountains. When they started getting diseases and food got scarce, the Jaguar Entity came to 'em and said it would take everybody to the moon 'til it found a new home for 'em on Earth. The High Chief was part o' the group that accepted the offer. Klara and the other ones stayed on Earth, migratin' to Germany."

"Quite fascinating. Our textbooks never went into that much detail. Then again, the old Elehominum and their envoys weren't interviewing them; they were thrashing them," reckoned Noah.

"How can yi be sure it's true and not lies? Navi'el seems dishonest," Piper said.

"I had solo guard duty at the lab in Noyeur Atlantis once. Was patrollin' the surgery hall when I caught 'em arguin' about the rift. Whole conversation was in Lu-narabik," evidenced Commander MacGregor, shifting their travel onto a construction site. "Not saying I'm the most fluent guy in their language, but I know enough to get by. It's a requirement for anybody coming into Noyeur Atlantis."

"I couldn't care less about their petty family feuds. I'm more interested in this 'Jaguar Entity'. I'm sure it's his trump card," Julien purported.

Gazing at the moon, Commander MacGregor's voice softened. "Haven't got a whole lotta intel on it, truthfully. No Commando's seen the ruddy thing, but I've heard the High Chief praying to it on nights when the moon is full. He asks it for guidance and wisdom. Might as well be his spiritual advisor, with how much he confides to it about his conflictin' morals."

"Maybe he'll have a change of heart," reevaluated Piper.

"Or maybe he'll beg for forgiveness like most cowardly ninnies do on their deathbeds," Noah said, drumming his fingers on the wrecking ball of a crane.

"I wish for every sinner to correct their wrongs and work to gain the Lord's favor, except him," evangelized Sister Agnieszka. "It is not my place to pass judgement; that right alone belongs to the Lord, but I believe he is unforgivable. Repentance will not wipe the black stains from his heart, nor will it restore the lives he has taken. His corner in Hell will be the hottest."

"Wouldn't have expected to hear so much damnation talk from heroes. Guess everybody's got a wee mean streak in 'em, even the do-gooders," Commander MacGregor ridiculed, veering onto a tarred walkway that fed into a backstreet.

Blair gave him a second smack. "Still runnin' that mouth, tellin' us about stuff we ain't asked for. Keep at it and I'll knock those yellow teeth down your throat."

"You're steady puttin' your scuzzy mitts on me, and it's pissin' me off, girl. That wasn't part of the deal," objected Commander MacGregor, turning around to face his abuser.

"No hands, no problem. How would ya like it if I put these feet through your skull," Blair tendered.

"I wouldn't take the bait. She hits hard and is handy with guns. Might be easier if you just zip it," spurred Noah.

"C'mon then, get me outta these cuffs. I'll show ya what the fightin' Irish is all about," Commander MacGregor raved, trying to rip apart his chain links. "I ain't your punchin' bag, ya mad backwards sewer rat."

Julien skirred between them. "Take a chill pill, both of you. Give the pettiness a rest, or I'll…"

A dreidel, coasting on a spill of bourbon, hushed his ultimatum. It tapped against his left loafer.

"I dunno what that is, but I already distrust it," said Blair.

"It's the main piece to a children's game played during Hannukah," Sister Agnieszka educated, collecting the four-sided top. "Each side has a letter of the Hebrew alphabet."

"Rabbi Tov loved playing it. He was the only Jew in Cumberchester Heights who could afford the pieces," circulated Piper.

"Which means we can't be far from where he taught," Julien intuited, shining his flashlight onto the backstreet's largest building.

The erection of basalt and chalk was encircled by citrus strainers and spoons. Barrels of brandy blockaded its rampway. Garlic plants punctured its spotty windows, tangling their leafy ropes throughout the forgotten property. Spider webs cocooned its gambrel roof. Ravens perched on its shingles, cawing at the torch's brightness.

A doorless, white stone cabin was to the distillery's right. Two poles displaying iron carvings of six-pointed stars were installed on its corner posts. Walnut Holocaust remembrance plaques flew around them. The windowsills were upraised, blinds flapping in the night's sporadic breezes. Pale green fog seeped out of the unsecured openings.

"I can sense the spiritual energies haunting Ner Tamid. Evil's flourishing on its grounds," Noah said.

"Another fight with a loved one," regretted Piper. "When will it end?"

Blair flipped the safety lock off of the Luger, yellow bands of electricity wreathing her ankles. "We'll take him out quickly. We got the numbers advantage, and a gun. He'll be a piece of cake."

"I am afraid you are wrong; this will be anything but easy," Sister Agnieszka diverged. "Do not forget: Rabbi Tov was a psychic. He's likely ten steps ahead of the curve. I fear this will be our deadliest challenge yet."

Sighting a cheese grater on the ground, Julien tucked the flashlight in his armpit and picked it up. He then slashed across the knuckles of his free hand. His self-mutilation sparked outrage.

"Good grief, this kid's a masochist," cringed Commander MacGregor.

"Mr. Preux, please explain your actions, lest I am to assume that someone has been a terrible influence on you," Sister Agnieszka probed, glancing suspectedly at Noah.

"I didn't tell him to hurt himself, miss, honest," disavowed Noah.

Rather than respond, Julien disregarded the commotion. He instead envisioned himself in chemistry class at Frederick Douglass High, weighing a spiky tablet of titanium. Picturing its bleached silver color and rough texture, his thoughts materialized and the low-corrosion structural metal hovered over his head.

"Wow, didn't kna yi could dee that," said Piper, watching as Julien's arm frothed and transformed into a glistening sledgehammer.

"Bravo, Mr. Preux," Sister Agnieszka commended. "I see you have proper justification for harming yourself. I must confess: I was unaware that the Goldevoire grace had such unique properties."

Julien hurled the cheese grater at a barrel, killing a sneaky doomsday mouse. "This is Welder Mode. I can use any one of the Seven Metals of Combat to make my arms a melee weapon, so long as I'm in a heightened state of pain and focused on a specific metal."

"Your little tricked-out arm is nice, but it won't mean nuttin' if the rabbi can predict your moves," undermined Commander MacGregor.

"There's an easy fix for that: we won't let him take a breather. He can't read everyone's minds at once," Julien predicated, starting for the synagogue.

Blair frogmarched Commander MacGregor behind him. "You're who should be goin' in first, not none of us. Ya might've gotten a pass earlier, but don't get it twisted; I'll happily use ya as a human shield."

"May the good elements ensure we are victorious," implored Sister Agnieszka, trailing Noah and Piper as they walked onto the backstreet.

They entered. The synagogue's interior was one large room. A heart-shaped entry alcove, with a rope-pull hanging down from the steeple above, opened out into a nave where softwood pews offered seating for about thirty people. A man in tattered black robes and a matching yarmulke shambled at the front of the nave, igniting emerald flames on the eight candles of an ivory menorah. His face was a mesh of burned skin and misshapen cartilage.

Tapping his flashlight on the back of a pew, Julien tried to get the man's attention to no avail.

"Rabbi Samuel Tov, former envoy of Edenshire Academy," Sister Agnieszka addressed. "You have been corrupted. Navi'el's ungodly curses manipulate your body. It is our sworn duty to neutralize the threat you've become."

"It's for the best," said Piper.

Noah closed a siddur that sat on a pew's armrest. "We'll put you out of your misery, give you the peace in death we couldn't in life."

"You think now, to betray me," Rabbi Tov slandered, his tired voice an echoing whisper. "I had high hopes for you."

The spellbound clergyman hurriedly turned, pointing the menorah as its handle lengthened into a staff. A green laser drilled through Commander MacGregor's forehead. The flame of a candle extinguished. He fell, dying with his eyes open and locked on Julien.

CHAPTER X

Commander MacGregor's fatal wound steamed. Fizzing, it gaped and gushed brain fluid. The teeth of those handcuffs sawed the porcelain floor, scraping redone ceramic varnishes until a final convulsion. A case of pink pills had fallen out of his jacket's breast pocket during the shakes. Stiffening, he wet himself. The urine stain slathered his pelvic region, and stunk strongly of ripened fruit.

"You don't get cool points for murdering a guy with his hands behind his back," Julien said, leaning down to close the Commando's eyes. "Didn't even have the decency to give one of your own a fair chance to defend himself before you turned on him."

"Navi'el robbed Rabbi Tov's grave, yet could not steal his integrity," reproved Sister Agnieszka.

"And that's why it ain't no honor among thieves," Blair abhorred, firing the Luger at him.

Fearless, Rabbi Tov did not flinch as the bullet zinged past his enfolded ear. Upraising the menorah, he lasered a hole in the roof of Ner Tamid.

Blair clicked the trigger again, but the Luger was depleted of ammunition.

"Your criticisms hold no bearing or weight; I foresaw MacGregor's intention to switch sides. He assumed it would result in his mother's freedom. Little did he know, she's been dead for days in Noyeur Atlantis. The cannibals are feasting on her lard."

"She had nothing to do with any of this," scolded Julien, readying his guards. "For every boy that loves his mama, I'll punish you and Navi'el."

"How heartwarming. Do give her my regards, should you two cross paths in the afterlife," Rabbi Tov hectored, shooting a laser at Julien.

"Move outta the way," apprised Piper.

Julien dodge-rolled, relocating himself to the footrest of a pew. His flashlight skidded under a cupboard that contained Torah scrolls. Gliding ghostlike across the floor on the toes of his tan Chelsea boots, Rabbi Tov met him with a punch to his ear. He proceeded to apply a headlock, and paddled him with the menorah's blunt end.

"Not ganna let yi ruin my old envoy's reputation," Noah spurned, dashing and spitting spears of ectoplasm.

Rabbi Tov casually leaned to his right, avoiding the flurry of sharp, purple shafts. "You forget my extraordinary talents of mindsight, Mr. Satterly."

Sinking his hips and accelerating speed, Noah telegraphed a tackle.

"Hard of hearing, it seems," traduced Rabbi Tov, launching Julien head-first into his classmate.

The boys' skulls bashed and they plopped onto their stomachs, groaning.

Rabbi Tov straightened his yarmulke. "Would any of you like to try your hand? I cannot fault you if you decline; little girls have no place in fights. Graces do not change the fact that you are the weaker sex. Fate has foretold your roles."

"Big talk for a dead guy," Blair said, discarding the unloaded Luger. "Me and my ladies ain't no housekeepers or cooks. Them old timey beliefs gonna get you murked, again. We some real-deal scrappers, believe that."

The female trio rushed Rabbi Tov. He sidestepped to avoid the electrified push-kick Blair meant for his chest, and bobbed out of reach of Sister Agnieszka's nunchaku swings.

"Back in the ground yi go," enacted Piper, wiping sweat from her brows and slapping the ground to cultivate a stretch of quicksand.

Rabbi Tov shot two lasers to vaporize the glutinous soil. Seeking to exploit the momentary distraction, Sister Agnieszka tried to lash him at a lateral angle. He dodged and walloped the nun with his menorah. She went wobbling between two pews due to the blow's forcefulness, the candle cups leaving an impression on her cheek.

Blair threw another kick. Without looking, the treacherous theologian caught her foot before it could touch his porky neck. Piper was given a boot to the face for her attempt at baseball-sliding into his shin.

"What a pity it must be, realizing that you and your classmates are not the warriors your envoys imagined," Rabbi Tov demeaned. "Though I assume this position within Edenshire Academy gave you a purpose. What was a fatherless roughneck like yourself doing before becoming a graced child?"

"Thought you could read minds. Isn't it obvious?

I was lookin' for your grave, so I could spit on it," riposted Blair, balancing on one foot.

Stretching her leg to her shoulder, Rabbi Tov gave her no option but to perform a backflip.

"You're very nimble," he said. "Was it your drug addict of a mother who taught you these stunts? I'm sure she did many erotic contortions for the slumlords that aided her habits. Such indecency, all to get one teeny prick of a heroin needle."

"Don't you ever talk about my mum. You dunno what me or her have been through," prohibited Blair, attempting a roundhouse kick.

Rabbi Tov slung her toward Julien and Noah, who were staggering to their feet.

"Your life of arrest warrants and school suspensions aren't worth my talents. I see the future, and none of you are included. Guess who is the first to die an excruciating death."

Rabbi Tov projected a foggy laser at Blair. Leaping in front of her, Julien blocked the lethal light beam with his titanium arm-hammer. The metal simmered on contact, whistling as green particles exploded along its ridges. None did damage.

"Oh, majestic! A graced child is a graced child, even in an unwinnable contest," Rabbi Tov teased, snickering and swiveling his menorah.

Recuperated, Piper and Sister Agnieszka scurried to rejoin their allies.

"Read our minds all you want. We're not giving up easily," said Julien, spit-shining the hammer's head. "You'll have to earn any kills you get on us tonight."

"Man ain't nothin' special. If those psychic powers were legit, he would've known that Magdalene was gonna stir-fry him and Abigail," Blair denounced.

Rabbi Tov's laughter quieted. Freezing in mid-step, he clutched his menorah with both hands.

"Aw, did I strike a nerve? You were chattin' like a big-time drilla, 'til I brought up how you got cooked by her flamethrower," said Blair. "How'd that hot sauce feel?"

Slamming his menorah, Rabbi Tov generated a vibrational wave that flung the Elehominum and their envoy in opposite directions. Julien and Blair were blown behind a pew, while Sister Agnieszka, Noah, and Piper landed under the seats of the one diagonal to it.

"Dying gave me eyes on the inside," Rabbi Tov alluded. "How else would I know the lurking fear of unworthiness despairs Agnieszka nightly, or that you are with child and the leader of this class is its father? That which is unperceivable by mortal men is clear to me."

"Father Nigel would despise what you've become," faulted Noah.

"He'd remind yi of everything that our school stands for," Piper accorded.

"He will be my apostle in the High Chief's New World," preordained Rabbi Tov, angling his menorah skyward.

What remained of Ner Tamid's roof sunk inward, forming down-sloped rafters. Emerald-green shimmers overspread the night's starlight. Hovering, Father Nigel's corpse anchored onto a mudstone altar that spawned from the ground in the rear of the synagogue. The punctures Victoria's trident made in his chest were teeming with crickets. Their chirps were husky and discordant.

Noah and Piper covered their mouths, horrified.

"Unforgivable blasphemy," said Sister Agnieszka.

"This is where the buck stops. You won't be getting my or anyone else's forgiveness," Julien convicted, standing. "Killing one of your own is whack, but not really any skin off my nose. Messing with someone I knew personally will get you a grade A beatdown."

The crickets' unharmonious chirping intensified.

"What is it that you are waiting for then, my dear boy? Come and meet your doom head-on," solicited Rabbi Tov.

"You should've already seen me coming."

Vaulting over pews, Julien employed his arm-hammer to block and swat two lasers. He met Rabbi Tov at the altar and threw a haymaker. Swishing, his punch hit nothing but air.

"I could've ended your miserable existences seconds ago. You're still breathing because I want to give the High Chief adequate time to complete his rituals," Rabbi Tov avouched, thrusting his menorah at Julien's stomach.

Gaveling his titanium extension, Julien knocked the malevolent candelabrum out of Rabbi Tov's hand. "He can take as much time as he wants, but you won't be around to see anything other than a coffin's lid."

They battled, parrying each other's strikes. An eye poke tipped the exchange in the revolting rabbi's favor.

Blair sprang up and made a dash for Rabbi Tov's equalizer. Her fingertips had just prodded the hilt when it joggled and retracted to its owner.

"We mustn't take what does not belong to us,"

Rabbi Tov said, whacking her across the back with his menorah.

Slumping, Blair tensed her shoulder muscles. She jerked her bandana down, coughing up static. The electric bands that wreathed her ankles dematerialized.

"Students were well-mannered before Edenshire Academy outlawed corporal punishment," substantiated Rabbi Tov, preparing to attack again. "Traditions are traditions for a reason. Bad behavior will not be tolerated in the High Chief's New World."

Flicking his metallic wrist against the candle holders, Julien prevented the crazed cleric from landing a second blow.

"Are all psychics slower than snails, or is it just you?"

"Seems you have inherited your great-grandfather's biggest flaw: you're just as annoying as he was."

Julien and Rabbi Tov's war of words precipitated their fight's third round. They clashed, the recurrent grating of their respective weapons producing thunderous clangs. Julien avoided another eye poke, but grew exasperated in his unsuccessful attempts to club Rabbi Tov. Furiously panting, he had become sloppy and heavy-handed.

Bounding, Sister Agnieszka, Noah, and Piper inserted themselves into the mix.

"Yes, come with numbers. It makes no difference," welcomed Rabbi Tov, evading Julien's frustrated swings and flooring him with an upward swipe.

Noah, the first to reach him, blew black, smoggy breaths in his face. The ectoplasmic oxygen was fanned away by the menorah, and he was kneed in his chest. Winded, he teetered onto a pew.

Digging her nails into the ground, Piper summoned sanded thorns that hastily ensnared her former envoy's legs.

"I remember when you found that technique difficult to master. You were so disheartened, I was compelled to give you a passing mark on your fifth exam because I pitied you," Rabbi Tov smirked, shattering the granular binds with a tap of his menorah. "How do you feel now, knowing it is utterly useless?"

Inhaling the dust and extending his arm, he scudded to Piper. A one-handed push drove her to the altar.

"We're the only two left standing," said Sister Agnieszka. "You may be able to read minds, but I haven't forgotten how your power works: you can't predict a person's actions before they have a thought."

"I could be legally blind, and you would still be outmatched, woman," Rabbi Tov gloated, tightly clasping the menorah's base and spinning toward her like the deadliest of toy tops.

Whipping her nunchucks, Sister Agnieszka hooked an unlit candle holder. She crouched low and allowed the momentum to propel her into a groin punch, landing the first successful strike on him. Reeling, he fell to one knee.

"Seems to me you're losing your touch, sir."

Rabbi Tov threw the menorah at Sister Agnieszka, forcing her to scurry behind a pew. It returned to him like a boomerang.

"Such an obnoxious woman, speaking when you aren't being spoken to. No wonder you haven't found a husband, or even a man worth his salt to court you.

You suppress your desires to be a mother by being an envoy to these inept children. Your feeble sanity and will to live will decay when I terminate them."

"Yeah, yeah, shut up. You ain't killin' nobody."

Blair had spoken, but it was a dizzy Julien who arose.

"I intended to kill you last. Your classmate's arrogance has moved you up my list," Rabbi Tov adjudicated, rushing him.

He pinned Julien against a wall and held the menorah under his chin. All eight candles reignited.

Then, something unprecedented happened.

Julien's arm-hammer became infused with lava. Red and orange streaks bedazzled the titanium, boiling.

Perplexed, Rabbi Tov studied the altered metal. "What is this?"

"Unforeseen circumstances," bemused Sister Agnieszka, lassoing him with her nunchucks.

Julien swung, ramming the hammer's head into Rabbi Tov's abdomen. Molten semifluid devoured his entire torso. Sister Agnieszka tugged on the handlebars of her nunchucks. The backbone addition acted on its own accord, strangling and decapitating him. His headless body dropped to its knees, rigid.

"You ain't a Vulcanold," Blair said, catching the menorah. "How'd you use lava if it ain't your grace?"

"I haven't got a clue," professed Julien.

The fiery streaks dripped off his arm-hammer, pooling into a blobby spill. It coalesced and reshaped itself into a gem. Smoking, the colorful essence rocketed up and out of the synagogue.

"Two graces at once? That's unheard of," Noah

reported.

Sister Agnieszka sat the dreidel beside Rabbi Tov's head. "Actually, it isn't. When Elehominum die, their grace is secreted from their body so it may be recycled for the next user. It is not uncommon for a grace to temporarily bond itself to someone who had a connection with its previous user, especially if they require assistance. I would not expect you to be aware of this tidbit; some information is solely reserved for envoys."

"So, you're sayin' you knew this was bound to happen," construed Blair.

"These exact events? Absolutely not. What I'm saying, Ms. Bisping, is that I felt the presence of an unfamiliar but friendly graced child among you when you came aboard the boat," Sister Agnieszka simplified.

"Salvador's last gift," deciphered Julien, his arm reverting to its normal state. "He wasn't kidding about wanting to share a leader's burden with me. It's like I had a piece of him with me this whole time. What I wouldn't give to thank him."

Mourning at the altar, Piper folded Father Nigel's hands over his wounds. "Don't forget there's someone else we should be thanking, too."

"Maybe we should scoop out those crickets," Noah said, limping to her side. "He hasn't been dead for more than a few hours. His body could be preserved a wee bit longer."

"What good will that do? It's not gan change us having two torn apart envoys," sulked Piper.

Ambling to the altar, Sister Agnieszka wrapped the two younger Elehominum in her arms. "You must understand, children: bodies are nothing more than shells. It is the human spirit that binds us to friendships and families. That, Ms. Woolgar and Mr. Satterly, can never be ravaged."

"Man had a reckless tongue," Blair pronounced. "You three must got the patience of Chinese monks, cuz I wouldn't have stood for him chattin' like that to me in a classroom. I had a go at my primary school teacher for far less."

"He was different when he was alive," quarreled an offended Piper.

"Yi can't judge the character of a reanimated person," Noah particularized. "Dead-riser hexes are fueled by negativity, like jealousy and hatred. When they bring someone back, it isn't the same person that died. They're the worst version of themself. It's why the Scarlet Gospels forbids us Grimemories from using them, unless we've got an envoy-approved reason."

"Yo, I wasn't tryin' to diss. I'm keepin' it a hundred; I wouldn't rock with anybody who thought that way about women," reemphasized Blair.

Lifting Father Nigel's sunglasses, Sister Agnieszka closed his eyes. "Long before becoming an envoy, Rabbi Tov's views were chauvinistic. He was a firm believer in traditional gender roles, and did not think kindly of those who deviated from them. The first class he mentored at Edenshire Academy was all-female. Those young women were fast learners and resilient fighters, not unlike the soldiers he and Father Nigel served with. He told me himself that they showed him how stupid he was."

"Everyone says or does something dumb at

some point, Bee," Julien said, easing his hand onto Blair's stomach. "Life's about growing and learning. Admitting that you were wrong is tough to do, but it's a big part in maturing."

Blair briefly laid her hand on his before pushing it away.

"We should give them both a proper burial in Blythe Gardens," recommended Noah.

"It's the least we could do for these old blokes," Piper sobbed, drying her tear-stricken face on Sister Agnieszka's cloak. "Can we?"

"I will leave that decision up to Mr. Preux," deferred the nun.

Julien nervously thumbed his scant chin hairs. "Please don't hate me for this, but I'd rather we keep moving. There's no way to gauge how far along Navi'el's plan is, so it'd be smarter to go to our school and get the Celortus' advice."

"Perhaps there is a suitable alternative," Sister Agnieszka mulled.

The crickets' chirps abated.

"I can charm the synagogue if you give me two minutes," negotiated Noah. "It'll hide the whole place, and seal the entrances. Usually lasts for a few hours."

"Do what you gotta do. We'll double back here after we stop Navi'el. We can have actual funerals for them once the world's secured," Julien compromised.

"What about MacGregor?" asked Blair. "We leavin' him here, too, or tossin' him on the street like a bum?"

"Yep, we'll keep him here so we don't draw any attention to this area," Julien concerted, reclaiming his flashlight.

"Sweet, I'll get everything sorted. We'll need to leave out so I can work without risking us being locked inside," said Noah.

They exited, stepping pitilessly over Commander MacGregor's body.

Pacing about Ner Tamid, Noah yawned ectoplasmic gases. His forefingers drummed on bricks at random, a festering, black gelatin loosening them. A mishmash of purples garnished the synagogue, coating it in a sticky adhesive. Rocking, the building vanished.

"You're an incredible wizard, bro," Julien edified, high-fiving him.

"I expect nothing less of Mr. Satterly, or anyone else doing unauthorized studies in the Library of Solstice's Restricted Area," said Sister Agnieszka. "He'll be able to tell me all about the things he learned whilst there, as I also expect a 20-page paper on the matter to be in my hand by Monday morning. No excuses, no extensions."

"But, but, miss," Noah faltered.

"Yi shouldn't have been breaking rules," indicted Piper.

"Ms. Woolgar is correct, and I don't want to hear another peep about it," Sister Agnieszka sanctioned. "You are an intelligent boy, with charisma and a thirst to drink from our school's fountain of knowledge. Those qualities, while great, do not give you the right to disobey."

"Won't happen anymore," said Noah, crossing his pointer and middle fingers.

Julien uselessly clicked the flashlight's power button. "I'm not asking for preferential treatment, but we can worry about punishments later. I want us to hurry and get going, it's just that this thing won't turn on."

"We don't need that anymore; we can use this instead," said Blair, elevating Rabbi Tov's menorah.

Julien rolled the flashlight toward Ner Tamid's invisible doorframe. "Suppose you're right. I'll leave this here in case Noah's charm is still in effect after we've taken down Navi'el. It could help us find the general vicinity of where the synagogue might be if the town warps itself."

"Normally, I would've banned the use of such a detestable device," Sister Agnieszka prefaced. "I'll allow its use under one condition: you must get rid of it before we enter Edenshire. I do not want to risk its evil influences befouling our school's hollowed grounds."

Blair nodded.

Head roving, Julien perused their squalid surroundings. "Glad we're in agreement. How much longer do we have to go?"

"We're in Bennington Court. That trail will lead us straight to school," shepherded Noah, pointing at an unpaved lane left of the synagogue's rear.

Clustering, they reinitiated their trek. Downed branches, cigarette filter tips, and squashed nightshade berries clogged the grassy entrance. Brown sugar aromas lingered in the air.

"Whole town's a trash dump," Blair said, first in line.

"Me and mam gan clean it up one day," undertook

Piper. "Has anybody else thought about what they'll dee once we're done?"

Noah swaddled himself in his cape, squinting at the numbers and lambda symbols. "Still got the coordinates of Quran, Atlantis' capital city. I'll be visiting our pals Cain and Umar regularly. I'm sure they've got some wicked magic tricks they can teach me, and vice versa."

"I will be an envoy for the foreseeable future. No exotic holidays for me. Edenshire is my home," said Sister Agnieszka.

"I'd planned on visitin' my nan in Cyprus to tell her about these last few days. Old bird loves one thing more than booze: magic stories," Blair preluded, leading them into a dense brush. "But I think she and me'll be havin' one of them serious talks about life and growin' up now."

Julien, in a botched scramble to monitor her stomach growth, tripped over a shrub. He caught himself on what he soon discovered to be the boots of a hanged Commando. His laces were bloody and double knotted together.

"Ugh, disgusting," Julien rued.

"God, you're the clumsiest guy on the planet," opined Blair, turning to him.

The menorah's green glow revealed not only the Commando's lifeless body to the oblivious others, but also that there was a carpenter's axe buried in his chest.

"Better him than us, innit," Noah maligned.

"Wonder who did this," said Piper.

"I won't go accusing anyone without proof, but I doubt we'll have to look that far," Julien gambled, scrubbing his hands on his jumpsuit's pants. "We've got some prime candidates for eyewitness testimonies."

Ten feet away, a freckled man wearing a coral poncho sat on a log, stirring a cauldron. A smaller figure, whose face was veiled by the hood of a yellow raincoat, was beside him.

"Keep your wits about you, children. Questioning suspects of a crime can be volatile," enlightened Sister Agnieszka, putting away her nunchucks.

Sneaking, they tiptoed to confront the persons of interest. Their footsteps were soundless until Noah stepped on a packet of saltine crackers.

"Come to arrest me, have you? That's fine, but you won't get any half-hearted apologies from me. Perv shouldn't have gotten handsy with my daughter," the man prattled, shoveling a spoonful of kidney beans into his mouth.

"Take it easy, big guy. We aren't arresting anyone," disconfirmed Julien.

"Yi did us a favor, slaughtering that pedo like a pig," Noah glorified.

Hearing their unexpected statements, the man craned his neck to face them and dropped the cauldron spoon in dismay. "Oh, my days! What the devil are you kids doing out here? Don't you know we're in the middle of a crisis? Thank the Lord above that the waters haven't swept none of youse up. Thank him doubly for not letting those wacky officers do youse any harm."

"I am a woman of the cloth, so believe me when I tell you that the Lord's good graces protect these children in more ways than you could ever imagine," said Sister Agnieszka.

The sugary scents of the beans wafted under the Elehominum's noses, making their famished stomachs grumble.

"Sure, I believe you, but I'm naturally a worrier. I've always taken care of my fellow townies," the man proclaimed, retrieving a plate of sausages from behind the cauldron and distributing them. "Name's Ronald Grimes and this is my little girl, Henrietta."

Julien, Blair, and Noah greedily munched their portions. Sister Agnieszka ate one half of hers, and stashed the other in her cloak. Piper politely refused the meat, informing Ronald that she was a vegetarian. Drifting off the log, Henrietta traded her a bowl of beans.

"Your generosity is appreciated, but I must ask you what happened," subpoenaed Sister Agnieszka.

"I was fixing me and Henrietta's dinner. The stove light randomly bursts and gas leaks everywhere. Henrietta comes running down the stairs, water shooting after her. I grab her and the food, and we leave. When we got outside, I was shouting for my neighbors to help me stop the flood, and that's when he came along," Ronald recounted, nodding at the hanged Commando. "Had a lady with him, too. She was asking me if I felt ill, and if I'd been getting enough sleep lately. That sket was just distracting me while he unbuttoned Henrietta's raincoat. Didn't take me long to realize their sick game. Gave the bloke open heart surgery with my neighbor's axe. The lady hightailed it while I was hanging him."

Blair picked her teeth clean. "What did this *lady* look like?"

"Super pale. White hair. Two-tone lipstick. Weirdest costume anybody's worn in Cumberchester Heights," characterized Ronald.

"Klara's on the move," Julien gleaned.

"She's slipperier than a normal snake," said Piper, eating the last of her beans.

Henrietta collected the empty bowl and returned to the log. A black butterfly emerged from a cocoon on the tree where the Commando was lynched, and flew onto her thumb. Lightning brightened the sky.

"Klara's heading for Edenshire. We can't let her find the Celortus," Noah appealed.

Ronald tightened the strings of his poncho. "No idea what a 'Celortus' is, but if you're talking about that school by the sea, I'd say you're right. Heard the gate creak half an hour ago."

"Thank you for the kindness, sir, but business calls. Get yourself and your daughter somewhere safe," commanded Sister Agnieszka, beginning the team's sprint.

Ronald bade them farewell, his fervent voice a bygone whisper.

They bolted to the trail's end, slowing at a tall, cast iron gate. Beyond its brittle bars sat their beloved Edenshire Academy. The magnificent, small-scale basilica's plum bricks were steeped in raindrops. A red moon loomed over its onion dome.

CHAPTER XI

Ordering the Elehominum to stand back, Sister Agnieszka plodded to the gate's entryway. She stuck out the arm on which she wore Ava's bracelet. Its wolf head charm emitted ultraviolet lines that silhouetted an otherwise undetectable, 50-mile border wall. The vertices mirrored the red moon. Shrinking, the whitish-blue lines broke apart and rearranged themselves into a scatter plot. Each sparkly dot spontaneously combusted.

"Klara must've gone somewhere else," the nun said. "Had she passed through here, her outline would've been shown. The Celortus specifically designed this barrier to alert envoys of any Mavkardia's presence."

"Are you sure? I mean, I never claimed to be a detective but there's a crapload of evidence to say she did," extrapolated Julien, investigating the ground.

Blair positioned herself beside him so the menorah's green lights could facilitate his analyses. "He's right. We can't ignore none of this stuff."

Shreds of the lace that threaded Klara's wedding dress peppered the moist dirt. Snakeskin sheddings neatly tied in bows ornamented freshly made sinkholes.

"That ugly hag's come this far, and decides to not go inside? She's got the attention span of a goldfish," Noah slighted.

"What if me mam came looking for us, saw Klara, and chased her away? That'd explain why she's gone," substantiated Piper.

"It's unlikely, unless some pretty heavy rainfall cleared her footprints," Julien rebutted.

"Enough speculation, children," offset Sister Agnieszka. "We'll get to the bottom of everything. Solomon has our answers. Follow me."

"Feels like our lil' story's comin' full circle, innit," Blair said, strutting in front of the nun.

Sister Agnieszka gently grabbed her by the wrist. "Please dispose of that, Ms. Bisping."

Blair blew out every candle. Wax trickled, melting the cups. Puffs of lime green smoke eddied from the wicks, spiraling into a fluffy cloud. She planted the menorah's hilt in the soil, and it burrowed underground.

"Good, we may now proceed," approved Sister Agnieszka.

Crossing the threshold to a triangular door, they entered Edenshire Academy. There were no muddy tracks on the cherry hardwood floor. The beige walls did not have a speck of dust on them. Both rhinestone chandeliers glittered just as they did before the Oath Keepers' latest siege.

"It's no different than how we left it," Piper determined, shutting the door.

Noah browsed the dictionaries of a weathered bookcase, his stomach's rumblings restored. "Up here is, aye. I vote we check the kitchen. We can inspect the pantries for fingerprints and eat some leftovers."

"Your hunger pains must wait, Mr. Satterly. We cannot afford to make a single detour on our way to the Library of Solstice," Sister Agnieszka disallowed, storming past the blue velvet steps of a pristine staircase.

The Elehominum followed her like ducklings led by their mother.

"I'm surprised you didn't tell us to not eat Ronald's food," said Julien.

"Was kinda unexpected, not gonna lie," Blair agreed.

Rounding the staircase, Sister Agnieszka stopped at a dual-gated elevator and pressed the third button on its rusted panel. "I've met him a few times, albeit under my many disguises. He's a selfless man, who reveres Christ. Had he been mind-controlled by demonic possession, I would've known."

The gates scissored open and they clambered onto the grass rug.

"So, is Solomon going to be okay with us coming in? It might just be an American thing, but our librarians ban kids that don't follow rules," Julien notified.

Noah whistled, looking to one of the elevator's tight corners to avoid eye contact.

"He is a timekeeper, not a librarian," rectified Sister Agnieszka. "Rest assured, Solomon will fulfill his duties. He'll also be delighted to know that Mr. Satterly will be helping him alphabetize the section for magically altered encyclopedias."

"But those were jinxed to constantly rearrange themselves; it'll take us weeks," Noah whined.

"You can thank your precursor Grimemories for that foolishness. Perhaps you'll teach future Grimemories that everything isn't a joke, and doubly when it pertains to Edenshire Academy," retorted Sister Agnieszka.

The elevator's clinking halted, and its doors squeaked open at a spacious, mint-green room. They filed inside, relishing the mild heat released by sapphire ceiling lamps. Glass-cased typewriters stood a foot in from the entrance. Books of varying widths were shelved on bamboo columns drizzled with rose petals.

"I've only been here once, but something about it feels so perfect," Julien savored, sniffing the air.

"Like being home," empathized Piper.

"The Library of Solstice tends to have that effect on people," Sister Agnieszka said. "It's a feeling of love and acceptance. Those sensations stroke the heartstrings of every individual who loyally practices the Wolven Way."

They passed multiple study tables, including the one that Julien smashed after Noah conducted a séance to contact Jean-Renee.

Sister Agnieszka stalled at the column behind the wood rubble, which was far wider than the previous ones. "Mr. Satterly, won't you do us the honors?" Noah reversed the order of the last three books on the middle row's left side. He then tickled their spines until they independently reestablished their original sequence. Warping, the column's appearance changed to that of a tall, flittering veil of silver. He peeled back its bottom right corner, revealing a cramped corridor paved in silt and yellow-green rocks. Smudged planks layered the low ceiling and walls.

"Wicked," Blair said, impressed.

Julien rubbed the veil. "What an ingenious hiding spot! Who would've expected there to be a hidden entrance here of all places?"

"Nobody, that's who," answered Noah. "This school's got limitless secrets, mate. Your head would explode if you overheard half the things I did while eavesdropping on conversations. Did you know that, one time at sunrise, Father Nigel was watching some Halle Berry film where she gets naked and his phone rang and…"

"Enough, Mr. Satterly. Any more self-incrimination and you'll be triple Father Nigel's age before you finish serving detentions," Sister Agnieszka warranted, crab-walking into the corridor.

The Elehominum mimicked her actions.

"Those are alkaline rocks. Yi can tell because of their colors," authenticated Piper, observing the ground. "The Stone of Golems tells us Geodactyls that our brains are full of alkaline rocks. S'why we've got such hard heads, me mam says."

"Isn't the Stone of Golems what Geodactyls use to get access to the part of the Library of Solstice that's only for them, kinda how the Mantrametalicus does for me and the other Goldevoires," Julien asked.

"Yep, and it can answer every question about any type of rock," sponsored Piper.

"I'd rather know why we're walkin' sideways," Blair preferred.

"The walls will cave in if we don't. It's a security measure to ensure that whoever's here is supposed to be, as they'd have been given explicit instructions on what to do," elucidated Sister Agnieszka, turning right at the corridor's end.

She passed through a wall. Trusting her spectral tactic, the Elehominum fearlessly crab-walked through the boards. The other side was a cosmic wonderland. The floor, though solid, was transparent and installed atop a range of stars. Shimmery books fit for giants stocked pearled shelves that were taller than skyscrapers. Outlines of vaguely humanoid figures pranced around the monumental structures, dusting the crannies.

"Wow, these dudes must be intergalactic ghosts from Pluto or something. They might have had some experiences with Navi'el that taught them how he can be beaten," Julien said, approaching the cleaners.

Soaring over the top of the farthest shelf, a life-sized paper airplane landed at his feet. It unfolded itself, becoming a large, upright sheet of hemp. Invisible pens colored a portrait of a yellow-eyed man whose body was made of clock gears. He stepped off the page, dwarfing Julien by four feet.

"What you see are not ghosts; they are the memories of the Wolven scholars chosen to be librarians, reenacting their last days in the Library of Solstice."

He spoke in a robotic, British accent.

"Oh, sorry. I'm still familiarizing myself with the ins and outs of Edenshire," Julien yielded.

"This is the Restricted Area of the Library of Solstice. Provide proof of your permission to be present, or I shall forcibly remove you," coerced the gear-man.

"At ease, Solomon," Sister Agnieszka refereed,

setting her hand on Julien's shoulder. "I gave these four graced children my blessing to enter."

Solomon curtsied. "Forgive my sternness, Headmistress Jędrzejczyk. The Celortus would undoubtedly decommission me if I were to be careless enough to continually fail the basest of my duties. As I am sure you are well aware, a student who shall not be named accessed the Restricted Area previously."

"Gee, who could he be talking about," Piper feigned.

Stuffing his hands into his pockets, Noah whistled again.

"You have my word: the student in question will assist you in organizational tasks to repay you for the headaches he's caused," brokered Sister Agnieszka. "I will sort his dates of service later, but your testimony on another matter is required immediately. Has anyone come to the schoolgrounds within the last hour?"

"I slumbered for the past hour, which is the daily minimum needed for my energies to function properly. While I wish I could be more helpful, it'd be wise of you to converse directly with the Celortus," Solomon said, turning toward the gigantic page that animated him. "I sense their presence in the late headmaster's bedroom. I will inform them that you and your wards seek an audience."

"Wait. You told us that those are memories cleaning the bookshelves, right?" questioned Julien.

"I did," Solomon corroborated, smoothing the page's corner creases.

"Jean-Renee Preux was my great-grandfather. If the Restricted Area has any memories of him, I think we should check to see if there's anything that we should consider," advised Julien.

Solomon pinched the page's top corners and looked to Sister Agnieszka.

"Yes, I authorize you to honor his request," the nun permitted.

"I will take you to the oasis where time defies logic."

Gears clinking, Solomon stretched the page as wide as his arms would allow and draped it around them. The bookshelves and their bygone cleaners were unexpectedly immersed in darkness. Stars exploded beneath their feet, blasting fireworks that heated the floor.

"Somebody should explain what's goin' on," screamed Blair.

"I'm as clueless as you are, but hold onto me so you don't trip and fall if you lose your balance," Julien coordinated, intwining her arm in his.

"Calm yourselves, children. I would see no harm come to you," said Sister Agnieszka.

A white sun restored the exclusive room's illumination. An hourglass revolved around it, names written in its sands. An aerial light screen replayed private matters, including Amelia writing Bible verses in Welsh and Blair's initial, regretful reaction to her haircut.

Solomon unwrapped the Elehominum and their envoy, and laid the paper like a strip of carpet. "Precisely on schedule."

The Restricted Area's architecture was replaced with full-length black mirrors seated upon a stream of red water. Throbbing bronze wires enwrapped their frame stands. Buoying clock hands engineered an echoing tick-tock.

"It's a chamber of secrets," Noah adulated, swirling his index finger in the stream's outer ripple.

Sister Agnieszka tapped her foot behind him. "Yes, Mr. Satterly, there are parts of Edenshire Academy that even *you* cannot worm your way into. To say this is the most secured location in the school would be an understatement."

"An appropriate description," graded Solomon. "The Hall of Remembrance is so secret, many students think it is an urban legend. Admittedly, the concept is outlandish. Who would fathom that a memory could be updated?"

"Let me get this straight: you're telling me that we can talk to someone's memory, and the stuff we say will become a new part of it," Julien cross-examined.

Blair untangled their arms and kneaded her forehead. "God, I'm getting' a migraine tryin' to process these mysteries."

"Allow me to show you how it's done," deputed Solomon, marching to a mirror.

His gears clanked and melded, transforming him into a singular cogwheel that clipped onto the frame's base.

"Solomon holds the keys to our school's most cherished memories. The Celortus embedded history in him, and you four will be among those few so fortunate to witness it firsthand," Sister Agnieszka dogmatized.

The black glass chinked. A bluish glaze repaired the damages. Whiteness overtook the colors. Condensation fogged the mirror until Solomon's gear spun, blowing air that nullified the aerosol. A young man who looked like a slightly older version of Julien stood clearly in the mirror's center. His outfit seemed to be a classic variant of the Edenshire Academy uniform. He wore a gray wool sweater over a white dress shirt. His black tie featured a golden wolf pin. The shirt's collar was neatly loosened, as if to parade the scars he had amassed. His corduroys matched the color of the sweater, and were starched to perfection.

"Marie wasn't joking; we look just alike," said Julien.

"Eh, wouldn't go that far, bruv. You're cute in a neeky maths tutor kinda way. Those cuts got him lookin' real manly," Blair disclaimed, pointing at the keloids on Jean-Renee's neck and upper lip.

"And he's got broad shoulders, so he looks a wee bit intimidating. No offense, mate, but you look friendly," prepended Noah.

"He's taller than you, too," Piper said.

"Enough comments on the appearance of Mr. Preux's great-grandfather," proscribed Sister Agnieszka. "Our goal is to gain insight, not compare and contrast their looks."

Jean-Renee's eyes bulged at the mention of his surname. He stepped through the mirror, speaking in thicker Kreyòl inflections than the incarnations of him that Julien had previously met.

"It has been a while since my family and I have spoken. I hadn't considered the possibility that one of my descendants could be an Elehominum, but I could not be prouder. What can I do for you?"

The Elehominum exchanged looks of confusion.

"I guess you're a little forgetful," Julien perceived.

"I'm your great-grandson, Julien. We already spoke twice: once in the main part of the Library of Solstice and again when I put the Atlantean crown on. I'm the current Goldevoire, remember?"

"Ah, but it is you who has forgotten how the Hall of Remembrance functions. Naturally, I only know what I did up to this age. Anything else would have to be told to me by a visitor," clarified Jean-Renee.

"Nobody's told him about the séance. Best we move on to the important stuff," Noah recapitulated, whispering into Julien's ear.

"Er, right, my fault," acquiesced Julien. "I'll get straight to the point: Klara von Schlange's been freed, and I need to know how to re-seal her in your amulet. Do I recite the inscriptions?"

"No, baz, that is a poem about its creation. All you need to do is trace a pentagram in the air," Jean-Renee said.

Noah eagerly shook his hand. "Excellent craftsmanship, old chap! Heretikrox might not be everyone's cuppa tea, but it fascinates me. I'm sure you can agree that dark minds like ours are underappreciated."

"Thank you, but I just welded the metal. My classmate, Conor Duffy, enchanted it," Jean-Renee corrected, retracting his hand. "He visits me regularly to tell me stories about what happened after this memory of me was archived."

"Mr. Satterly will be pleased to know that Mr. Duffy is one of the smartest Grimemories to have served the school," anticipated Sister Agnieszka.

Noah popped his collar, beaming. Repulsed by the wanton gloating, Piper pretended to stick her finger down her throat.

"As well as one of the most irritating and troublesome," Sister Agnieszka recommenced. "He was a student long before I was an envoy, but I've heard of his crude antics. Let this be a lesson to you: bewitching toilets to overflow and hiding an envoy's gradebook in Blythe Gardens are punishable offenses. Surely his classmate here can tell you the consequences are not worth the laugh."

"Not to knock his accomplishments, but Duffy's pranks are the least of my concerns. What we could really use are your tips for fighting Klara and Navi'el," quibbled Julien.

Jean-Renee's face scrunched. "You are asking for information I cannot give."

"Whaddya mean? You fought them both," Blair said.

"I did, but this memory of me was archived before that actually happened," explicated Jean-Renee. "Conor wasn't there when I sealed Klara, and he lost consciousness early in our fight against Navi'el. He does not know how it ended, therefore nor do I."

"Why did your envoys not visit you? They could have filled in the blanks," Sister Agnieszka presumed.

"I like to believe they would've, but Navi'el killed them," brooded Jean-Renee. "The only advice I can give is to go to your headmaster's bedroom. Conor tells me it's where a diary is hidden, and only envoys may find it."

Solomon's gear unclipped from the frame's base. Darkening, the glass fogged and disembodied hands reached out.

"It has been a pleasure. Thank you for these

memories," Jean-Renee ascribed, turning to re-enter the mirror.

"Yi might have something that your great-grandfather wants," hinted Piper.

Brain jogged by her suggestion, Julien gave him the zaternium engagement ring. "Oh, I almost blanked on it. We found this on Marie's body. Not too sure if that name means anything significant to this memory of you, but I could tell that she loved you unconditionally. Wouldn't be fair for us to keep it, so it's yours."

"I don't recognize the name, but somehow, I feel an emotional attachment I've never felt before," Jean-Renee whispered, taking the ring and marveling at its indigo luster. "Tell me, baz, could this be love?"

Those unearthly hands tweaked his sweater's sleeves, tugging him back into the mirror's domain.

"Well, what now?" asked Noah. "He gave bare bones answers to most of our questions. We're no better off than we were."

Solomon's gear disjointed, the multiple parts restoring his more mobile form. "I advise you to follow the lead he has given. This memory of Jean-Renee was not simply archived for pep talks and war stories, but for his uncanny instincts."

"So, we bail to Father Nigel's bedroom," Blair said. "Is there a shortcut, or do we gotta leave the way we came?"

"You can reach the late headmaster's bedroom by a quicker mode of transportation. Right this way," informed Solomon, lethargically guiding the visitors to a mirror adorned with wolf's fur.

"Unless I'm mistaken, this will bring us through

the other side of Father Nigel's vanity set," Sister Agnieszka postulated.

"You are not mistaken," verified Solomon, breathing heavily. "Though I must stress that the gateway between there and the Hall of Remembrance will be closed for, at the very least, an hour. Hosting Jean-Renee's memory was quite taxing on my facilities. I therefore must sleep. Should you need to return here, please do so how you entered."

"Thank you for your assistance. Rest well," Sister Agnieszka dismissed.

Solomon curtsied and dove into the stream, a splash of reddish waters proving its depth was deceptive.

"I haven't done mirror travel," weighed Noah. "Do we lean into the glass like they do in films, or is there a password we've gotta say?"

"We should be careful not to break anything. Seven years is a long time to have bad luck," Piper said.

"True, but there won't be nothin' to worry about in seven years if we're too late in stoppin' Navi'el and the snake broad," confuted Blair.

Sister Agnieszka took Julien by the hand. "Follow my directions, children. Grab onto the hand of the person beside you, and walk as if you're entering a normal, open space. Be confident in your strides; an envoy's bracelet may unlock this gateway, but it is the unquestionable faithfulness of wards in their envoy that enables the transportation. I ask you, my honorable champions: do you trust me?"

Widening, the mirror reflected the five of them.

"I trust you," the Elehominum warbled, linking their hands.

Random spurts of fireballs dribbled along the glass.

"Then let us walk by faith, not by sight," mobilized Sister Agnieszka.

Together, they entered the blazing mirror.

Their transmission to Father Nigel's bedchamber was instantaneous. Trekking onto the seared floorboards, they passed through the vanity's grand dresser like phantoms who were unimpeded by solid objects. Cinder residuum floated in the air, a chilling reminder of Magdalene's heinous assault.

"It's amazing being in a headmaster's room," Noah said. "Sister Agnieszka's is probably great, too, but this has gotta be more historic. Rabbi Tov and Abigail were burned alive here. Father Nigel blessed the holy water he sprinkled his bullets with here."

"How could anybody relax in this room, knowing what happened?" asked Piper, stroking the rosaries that hung on the crackled walls.

"Me and Bee have been here before, but I still can't explain its appeal or setup," Julien said. "There's a stash of filing cabinets in his closet. Add those to the list of stuff in this room I don't know the purpose of."

"Very disappointing. I hoped you vould tell me vat a blind priest vould need zat luxurious mirror for."

The black canopy curtains that screened the bed parted. Klara sat cross-legged on the mattress, drips of blood staining her velvety, gray skin. Agandeur Three-Chorus, the Atlantean hobgoblin, was nailed to the canopy's roof. Chunks of his kidneys clogged the zipper of his raggedy, olive trench coat.

"Maybe because it didn't belong to him, yi twit," insulted Noah. "We've had other envoys who weren't blind. Ever consider that, or is it too complicated of a concept for your little snake brain?"

"Not that it's any of your business," Piper supplemented.

"I zought zat ve vere friends," nettled Klara.

Stomping the ground, Blair sent up sparks and blew them out of her nose. "Keep up the jokes. We'll see who's laughin' when I put your head through one of these walls."

"How were you not detected by the school's barrier?" Sister Agnieszka catechized.

"Navi'el has already found and kidnapped zee Celortus. Edenshire's defenses are obsolete," alleged Klara. "I felt him nearby ven I met zat man and zee little girl in zee raincoat. Zee elixir you vatched me use gives me control over my snake form, but it hinders my senses. It tapered once I passed zee synagogue, restoring my legs and equilibrium. I felt zee full spectrum of his vitality."

"So, let me guess: you're planning on starting some supervillain marriage at our school tonight," Julien accused.

"Bet that's why she's wearing that musty wedding dress," said Noah.

"I vould not give Navi'el the pleasure of my caress, but zere is someone else I vill touch very intimately," Klara implied.

"We're doin' too much talkin' about this chick's sex life, and not enough fightin'," grumbled Blair, lunging at the eerily comfortable woman.

Julien restrained her. "Don't be so anxious, Bee. Remember, she has acidic spit."

"I am humbled zat I left a lasting impression," Klara vexed, her tongue slathering the blue-black corrosive over the teal that painted her top lip. "Do yourself a favor: listen to *our* boyfriend."

Blair squirmed, hollering profanities. Julien held her tighter.

"Don't take the bait; she's trying to get a reaction out of you."

"On zee contrary," disputed Klara. "I vill make you an offer zat you cannot refuse."

"Explain yourself, heathen," Sister Agnieszka obtruded.

"My people's deity vas zee Jaguar Entity, but it forsook zose of us zat did not keep its commandments. It cursed us to a lifetime of transformation to zee most deceitful animal: snakes. I vant vengeance," chronicled Klara. "None of you are capable of defeating Navi'el. I am zis vorld's only chance at salvation."

"I ain't heard no offer yet," Blair badgered.

"Zee red moon hangs low. I am at my most fertile. Let zee boy impregnate me," lobbied Klara. "He is zee second to be graced in zat bloodline, meaning it is favored by zee Celortus. Zee child vill have my immunities, and zee Goldevoire grace once I remove it from him. Dr. Jung developed a surgical process for zis very purpose. It is excruciating, but you vill live. A small price to pay for Navi'el's life, and at zee hands of your own seed no less."

"Gross, Julien's not some snake-shagger," Noah balked.

"Yi shouldn't be anyone's mam," decided Piper.

Sister Agnieszka raised her nunchucks, unblinking. "My ward will not be your sperm donor, Klara."

"Ya ain't got half a brain if ya think—"

"Deal," Julien complied, interrupting Blair's sentence as he unhanded her.

The Elehominum's eyes went wide with shock. None spoke.

"Mr. Preux, I explicitly forbid you from procreating with her," legislated Sister Agnieszka.

Wobbling, Blair clutched her stomach and painfully wailed. Noah and Piper caught her, preventing what was sure to be a forward fall.

"My mind's made up," Julien said, approaching Klara. "I'll do what's necessary to save the world. I just worry about what shape it'll be in with one Mavkardia ruling it instead of the other."

Klara uncrossed her legs. "I vill reset history's clock, so zat ve all have zee same opportunities. Zee banks and universities vill close. Militaries vill be disarmed, zeir weapons cast into zee oceans. Governments vill be disbanded. Ve vill rebuild zis society, and zose zat prosper vill have earned zeir place."

"I just want to know something first: why was I the only one who could hear your voice when we were on the street," asked Julien.

"My skin secretes a bonding fume. You did not notice because it has no color or smell. I marked you as my mate ven you came into my tent," Klara detailed. "Zee mark created a mental connection zat only ve can hear. I vill show you vat I mean."

Perverse demands and impassioned moans echoed in Julien's ears. Volume increasing, boastful claims of the carnal rewards Persians received for their membership in the Serpentine Sect followed. Julien covered his ears, wincing at the loudness.

"Why're we standin' around? She's hurtin' him, dammit," hassled Blair.

"I'm fine, stay where you are," Julien invalidated.

"How do we make this official?"

Skittering off the cashmere sheets, Klara swaggered to him. She let down her high ponytail, allowing the white hairs to mask her face. The diamond stud that pierced her lower, unpainted lip glistened.

"We consummate our arrangement," she cooed, tossing him onto the bed. "I vill conceive, and zee egg vill hatch in a day. Zee child vill be fully matured, and ready to take on Navi'el."

"You've got no shame doing it in front of everybody," criticized Julien, hands shakily reaching for his jumpsuit's zipper.

"I strike ven zee opportunity arises," Klara vaunted.

"So do I," said Sister Agnieszka, throwing her nunchucks.

The weapon struck Klara, and its knotted addition fastened around her throat. Gagging, she pawed futilely at the seventeen thoracic vertebrae.

"Now, Julien, use the amulet," Noah encouraged.

"Be careful, she might be faking," stressed Piper.

"I'll take care of that."

Shrugging her classmates off, Blair ran at Klara and belted her with an electrified knee to the spine. She keeled, mouth foaming expeditiously.

Slipping his hand into his pocket, Julien equipped Jean-Renee's amulet. Arm steadied, he traced a pentagram in the air. The five points whitened as they projected a spotlight of pastel ectoplasm. Grunting and floundering, Klara was vacuumed into the amulet's centerpiece.

CHAPTER XII

*J*ulien's hand trembled, the amulet throbbing in it like a beating heart. Gurgles and hisses rang from the five points, transmitting visible soundwaves. The Old Celortian text on its back bled ectoplasm. Gloppy, purple trickles clotted and spelled Klara's full name. Runover drip splashed onto Father Nigel's bedsheets, staining them. The amulet's tarnished gold chain links rattled, securing themselves around the centerpiece. Its erratic quivers ceased, evidently suppressed by the constriction.

"We've locked her away," Noah reveled. "Well done, chums."

"Sister Agnieszka's nunchucks are gone, too, though," said Piper.

"Sorry, I didn't realize the amulet's pull would suck everything inside it," Julien apologized.

Sister Agnieszka grabbed a floating pellet of ash and sprinkled the crumbles onto her face. "You couldn't have known, Mr. Preux. I will make do without them; chances are, Father Nigel has a loaded gun or two here somewhere. The Lord provides what is necessary."

"The closet's probably a good starting point," choreographed Julien, slinking off the bed. "It's where he kept his Army helmet. Remember when he talked about the war and showed us it, Bee?"

"Nah, bruv, all's I remember is how easily you were gonna smash Klara. You was pissy 'bout me and Paul bein' in a relationship before I knew you, but jumped at the chance to get up in her guts," Blair tongue-lashed.

"You can't compare those two; I was trying to give the world an insurance policy, not hookup with some fluke stick-up kid for my own pleasure," controverted Julien.

"At least Paul lasted more than a few seconds."

"And at least Klara thought enough of herself to sleep with a guy worthwhile."

"Neither of you should be criticizing the other. You both are guilty of violating one of Edenshire Academy's oldest educational decrees: no relations are to be had between active duty Wolven scholars," Sister Agnieszka pontificated, clapping in frustration. "Your exchanges were petty, tasteless, and unbecoming of a mother and father. Do better. Once we avert this crisis, healthy parenthood will be at the forefront of your responsibilities."

"If it's a girl, we should name her after Lilith, Adam's first wife. She's gotta be the most interesting woman in the Bible," proposed Noah.

"No way, she was a demon," Piper rejected. "But if it's a boy, we should name him after Rabbi Tov. He always wanted a son."

Ignoring their suggestions, Julien and Blair bitterly held each other's gaze.

Sister Agnieszka headed for the closet. "Mr. Preux and Ms. Bisping can pick their child's name on their own. What they choose to call it is none of our concern at the moment. Finding that diary is what's most important presently. Follow me."

Julien and Blair ended their staring contest, joining their classmates to fulfill the order. They jockeyed into the compact doorway of the broad recess, intent on not brushing elbows. Filing cabinets lined the plasterboard walls. Some were padlocked, and others were secured with push-button combination locks.

"I don't suppose there's a universal envoy numeric code that'll open these," said Noah, playing with a soldered lock's dial.

"Not to my knowledge, no," Sister Agnieszka disaffirmed.

"We should try birthdays or death years," recommended Piper.

Julien roamed the closet, pausing at a granite cupboard that featured a space for a hand impression above its handle. "Those won't help us with cracking this one. I'll eat my Burberry shorts if the diary isn't in here."

"What are ya waitin' for then, smart guy? Put your hand on it," Blair prompted.

Julien cut his eye at her, but did as she directed. Nothing happened.

"Your fingers really *don't* work magic, do they," mocked Blair. "Step aside. I'll do some shock therapy on it."

"You will not, Ms. Bisping. Use of your grace must be reserved for the battle ahead. Also, unlocking this cupboard may be simpler than you think," Sister

Agnieszka said, making her way to the site of intrigue.

Outstretching the arm on which her bracelet hung, she pressed upon the cupboard's hand-molded indentation. Elongating, the wolf head charm speared the keyhole and cranked. Rushes of smoke spurted from the opening.

"Elehominum were not meant to be privy to all the purposes of an envoy's bracelet," broached Sister Agnieszka, turning the handle. "Yet again this class finds itself in rare company."

There was one shelf inside the cupboard. A black book no larger than a pocket dictionary laid on it. Color-coded wolf pawprints were engraved on the cover. Its spine was tagged with holographic runes.

Inner strip light fixtures glinted to life, unshrouding the tactical supplies hidden by the smokiness of the cupboard's depths.

"We've hit the mother lode," Noah rooted, counting the assorted sub-machine guns and bandoliers beneath the shelf. "I doubt the Terminator had this big of a selection to choose from, man."

"Aye, I think yi might be right," said Piper.

"Don't go celebrating just yet," Julien discouraged. "It'd suck for us to assume that's the diary, only for it to end up being someone's essay drafts."

Sister Agnieszka opened the book, flipping through its pages of angelic artwork. "Mr. Preux speaks the truth. We mustn't get our hopes up."

"Don't tell me we did all this just to find a couple mediocre sketches," Blair repined.

"Na, I'm seeing more and more Old Celortian written on these pictures," reassured Noah, reading alongside Sister Agnieszka.

"Really, what's it say?" Piper hounded.

Sister Agnieszka stopped on a page that was aglow with burning letters. "Cthygonaar murak lizbet ya'har. Unigah spek da'unz lechautzu'vup Jean-Renee humb Navi'el. Ur natakarac Blaque Gaald zuri Goldevoire mahat laza."

"I heard my great-grandfather's name, and Navi'el's," boomed an overexcited Julien.

"This says, when they fought, neither was the victor. It was a draw," Sister Agnieszka translated. "However, Jean-Renee was on the verge of winning. Had he first studied the Black Gold Mode of his grace, he would've been immune to the metal poisoning it brings."

"Black Gold? He didn't tell me there was a level stronger than Welder Mode," cerebrated Julien.

Noah passed Sister Agnieszka an MP5 and a bullet belt. "And Father Nigel didn't tell us he had these Rambo guns."

"Sounds dangerous," Piper gauged. "Maybe Jean-Renee didn't want you to go hurting yourself."

Scanning the lighted text, Sister Agnieszka mumbled more Old Celortian before giving another translation. "Black Gold Mode is, apparently, activated when a wounded Goldevoire is in a state of rage. If he or she manages to focus that aggression on a specific target, they will channel the Seven Metals of Combat simultaneously. Gold will be the overall composition, but the strengths of lithium, titanium, copper, zinc, mercury, and silver will also be applied. The user must have a genuine desire to kill. This rabid urge will manifest itself in black spirals that layer the gold."

"Ah, so, no more of this lil' Mr. Nice Guy routine. You gotta really turn your savage up, really mean to hurt people. It's about lettin' your darkest side take over," kindled Blair. "I'm not convinced you've got it in ya."

"I'll prove I do whenever we find Navi'el," Julien pledged.

"There may yet be a safer way to win, one that does not involve tactics that will anger the Celortus," opposed Sister Agnieszka, taking the amulet from him. "We will seek their counsel."

She placed the amulet and the diary on the shelf and, as if her actions were the final requirement of some enigmatic spell, the cupboard morphed into a carbon ladder. It led up to the ceiling, where an orange portal swirled.

"Lord have mercy," Sister Agnieszka gasped. "This is extremely unfortunate."

"Why, where's this ladder go," asked Julien.

"To the lunarium," Sister Agnieszka said.

"Which is," prodded Blair.

"A place where yi can get a closer view of the moon," Noah encapsulated.

"That's only partly true, Mr. Satterly," refined Sister Agnieszka, strapping the bullet belt to her chest. "It is actually Edenshire Academy's entry point to the moon, where envoys formally take their oath to be sworn in by the Celortus. An outsider has discovered it."

"Navi'el," Piper named.

"But of course, Ms. Woolgar," legitimized Sister Agnieszka.

"Then let's not keep the wasteman waitin'," Blair

inspirited.

Julien gripped the side rungs, commencing their ascension. "Finally, something we can agree on."

They scaled the ladder, venturing into the orange unknown. Swooshes and crackles echoed around them. The temperature alternated between bitter cold and summery heat as they neared a tunnel stippled in salt. Julien, captain of the climb, was first to behold the moon's mind-boggling terrain.

Sprawled puddles glowed yellow, reflecting the jaguar star constellation in the cosmic darkness above. Queen ants birthed broods of worker ants in craters. White lilies flowered the surface, opening and closing to reveal rows of twisted, red thorns. One towering sequoia tree was planted in a plot of soil. The branches bore jet-black apples. Four limp bodies, each submersed in a thick sap and masked by burlap bags, were hogtied to its trunk. Barefoot, a revamped Navi'el sung Lu-narabik hymns to the captives.

He was shaved bald, and donned a peregrine feather headband. Bronze-plated arm bangles squeezed his toned biceps. His nipples were pierced with flint rings. He wore a tattered, brown loincloth that was knotted at the sides, and bedecked with beads. Rosettes were branded on his back and legs.

"This joker's had a makeover," Blair fomented. "He can tattoo as many jaguar spots as he wants on himself, but it ain't gonna matter. Man's washed."

"Your henchmen are dead. Surrender peacefully, or I will shoot," imposed Sister Agnieszka, taking aim.

Navi'el casually faced them, his saffron eyes glimmering like a supernova's light. "I caution you to not be too trigger-happy. Then again, you've spent the night hurting people you claim to care about, so what's a few more?"

"Yi take that back! We did what we had to, not because it's what we wanted to do," Piper absolved.

"I'm sure they'd rather die a bajillion times than serve the likes of you, anyway," reputed Noah.

"Let's ask these poor, defenseless people," Navi'el said, pulling a bag off one person's head.

Unconscious, Southside P snored.

"What, ya expect me to not apply pressure cuz you snatched up my dumb ex-boyfriend," discounted Blair.

"Excuse the low value of my catch; I would have taken your mother had I known which alley she purchased drugs in tonight," Navi'el goaded, removing another person's bag. "I am sure this one, though, will be of much higher regard than the last."

Ellis blinked heavily and yawned, as if she was succumbing to the effects of a prescription-strength sedative. Gasping at the sight of her mother, Piper inched forward but Noah held her back.

"Get a hold of yourself. Your emotions are gan get everybody killed, including your mam!"

"Sound advice. I wonder if you'll be able to maintain your newfound rationality once you see who this is," baited Navi'el, unmasking a third person.

It was a lean man with a thinning combover wearing an eyepatch. His head lolled onto Ellis' shoulder as he sleep-talked about Atlantis.

Noah swallowed hard. "Uncle Jonty."

"Yes, your only blood relative who loves you," Navi'el crooned. "Without him, you'd truly be an orphan."

"I've had enough of you trying to traumatize my classmates," intervened Julien.

"You have the animosity of someone who feels like they've been sorely overlooked. Trust me, I did not forget about you," diagnosed Navi'el, exposing the final hostage's identity.

Emmanuel, Julien's cousin, wheezed in his sleep. Half of his dreadlocks had been torn out at their roots.

"Caught him hiding on a beach in Port-au-Prince after he stole a tourist's wallet. The locals thought I was some vengeful spirit come to punish him for his misdeeds," Navi'el said, tapping the unruly boy's bloodied scalp. "I would have preferred to take your parents, but I know he means more to you. Deep down, he's who you wish you could be like."

Quivering, Julien's hands balled into fists. "My family's got no part in your beef with Edenshire, neither does anyone else who isn't an Elehominum or envoy."

"I assumed seeing your cousin beaten and bruised would bring out the fighter in you," delineated Navi'el. "You're no stronger than you were when you fought Emily. This school's preparation is laughable. What value do you think there is in fraternizing with these white devils?"

"These are my people," Julien proclaimed.

"They enslaved your people, raped mine out of existence," thundered Navi'el, his voice loudening with resentment. "Your ancestors fought in the Haitian

Revolution. They would be sick to their stomachs if they saw you siding with the oppressors. Has history taught you nothing about the ruthlessness of the Europeans?"

"I'm a European and damn proud of it; why don't I come over there and see if ya got the balls to say that garbage to my face," Blair challenged.

She took a single step and froze. A gush of clear liquid ran down her legs. She fell onto her buttocks, grunting and sweating profusely. Her stomach expanded to the diameter of a basketball.

"Dear God, her water's broken," announced Sister Agnieszka, dragging Blair toward the entry portal.

The orange vortex shrank to a decimal with a flick of Navi'el's wrist. "Is this the beginning of your forfeit?"

"Dream on, juicehead. Me, Piper, and Noah got what it takes to put you away for good," Julien said. "If we're really on the moon, then you made it easy for us to get some reinforcements. Our Kindred Spirits are gonna rip the skin right off your bones."

Cupping their hands to their mouths, the three of them howled in harmony. Bursts of color streamlined from their chests, shaping their spiritual protectors. The first to fully materialize was the smallest. Jagged rock fragments razored its brown, gravel-caked fur. Next was a purple wolf with hollow eye sockets and a see-through body, allowing all to watch as its organs pulsated. The final to emerge was the pack's alpha. Completely gold, its sawtooth fangs twinkled brighter than the stars. Two sets of sputtering drills protruded from its flanks.

"Cute, but I'm afraid your toothless puppies

are not good enough," depreciated Navi'el. "I, too, have a spirit guide, and these infantile pets pale in comparison to its greatness."

"Hurry, children, the very fate of humanity hinges on your victory," Sister Agnieszka said, spreading Blair's wavering legs.

"Make him your chew toy," sicced Julien.

The golden wolf led the charge, its pack mates following suit. Their combined growls muffled Blair's anguished cries, and Sister Agnieszka's directions for her to push. Lunging at Navi'el, the fantastic beasts hit a checkered forcefield.

"My life is thread upon your loom. Wash me in the light of your moon," he prayed, a sprouted, cliff-dense bloodstone citadel elevating him. "O Ya-heemah, Great Jaguar Entity, hear my call of distress. Protect me from those would seek to harm your last, true devotee."

The jaguar constellation exploded. Starry debris fell, encircling the cliffs. They reconnected with each spin until Navi'el's aforementioned god was once again made whole.

"The citadel, the cliffs," deliberated Julien. "They're what Umar saw in his vision."

Pouncing to Navi'el's side, the celestial cat was twice as large as a normal jaguar. The orange rosettes on its shadowy fur were ever-changing in shape, and expelled black halos. Its eyes were moonlit oceans.

"Ya-heemah has answered my prayer. This battle's unwinnable for you," Navi'el doomed.

Julien looked at the tree-bound hostages, and then at Sister Agnieszka as she attempted to deliver the baby. "We've beaten the scariest monsters anybody could ever imagine. There's no reason to believe we can't overcome these odds."

"How arrant mortals can be, tirelessly meddling in transcendental affairs their lowly brains cannot begin to comprehend," reprimanded Ya-heemah, its whispery voice both masculine and feminine. "Though an Elehominum you three may be, your bones break as easily as anyone else of your ilk. You are not special; you were merely chosen to be the Celortus' last line of defense against High Chief Navi'el. You will not prevail."

"It can talk," Noah said sheepishly.

"Consider yourselves fortunate to hear these inhuman utterings before breathing your last breaths."

Springing from the citadel, Navi'el and Ya-heemah ran through the forcefield.

"If they get a running start, so do we," insisted Julien, rallying Edenshire Academy's infantry.

The Kindred Spirits stampeded to Ya-heemah. It flipped and continually rotated, its tail sharpening into a stake. The purple wolf's left paw was spiked when Ya-heemah abruptly plunged, the sting causing it to cry tears of ectoplasm. The gold and brown wolves came at the spotted titan from both sides, intending to bite its throat. Tail unpinning from the purple wolf's paw, it reeled and paced, daring them to mount an offense.

Navi'el jumped over Noah and Piper, kneeing Julien in his face. The blow's velocity had him sidewinding toward the patch of thorned lilies. Neck propped against the rim of a crater, he watched Noah and Piper narrowly evade orange stardust sprays courtesy of Navi'el's birthmark.

"I gotta get up, they won't beat him alone," Blair coached, moaning and thrashing.

"You are in no condition to fight, Ms. Bisping," said Sister Agnieszka. "Your classmates will not lose. They'll rise to the occasion, because Julien's resolve is infectious."

Volts shot up Blair's knees, frying her socks.

Rolling onto his side, Julien swiped his knuckles across a lily's thorns to reopen his wounds. Blood jetting down his fingers, he sat up and spat out his front teeth.

"Dude hits like a truck, but you know what? The Elehominum who were here before me didn't give up, and neither am I."

Julien sprinted, a gold nugget orbiting his head. Counting to ensure his blood loss was equal to the metal's atomic number, he thought of Blythe Gardens and the poor maintenance of Jean-Renee's grave. Envisioning himself cutting away the weeds that obscured his great-grandfather's iconic name, he activated Welder Mode with two golden sickles.

Navi'el refocused the sprays at him. "So good of you to join us."

Julien dove under those dazzling discharges, swinging his sickle tips at the High Chief's ankles.

Navi'el jumped, stomping onto Julien's flexed wrists.

"Let's see how your gymnastics fare when me phantoms come alive," Noah touted, puffing out sword-wielding ectoplasmic beings lathered in oil and smoke.

Navi'el hopped back and mowed down the apparitions, horizontally spraying.

Clambering to a vertical footing, Julien told Piper to follow his lead. The plan of action, however, came to a standstill when Ya-heemah leapt in front of them.

"Your tenacity is exceptional, but will be your downfall. Blame the Celortus for feeding you the delusions that you ever had a chance at succeeding," it trivialized, raising one robust arm. "Welcome to the extinction of humankind."

The Kindred Spirits bounded to the Elehominum's aid. Clamping its jaws onto Ya-heemah's forepaw, the purple wolf tore muscle from bone. A line of ants scavenged the meat, undeterred by the ear-splitting combinations of barks and roars. The brown wolf headbutted the jaguar, staggering it. The golden wolf sank its fangs into its neck, chewed, and flung it toward the tree.

Ya-heemah climbed the branches, and the Kindred Spirits relentlessly pursued.

Their path cleared, Julien and Piper were appalled to see what that brief interlude had permitted. Palming his cranium, Navi'el brutalized Noah with forearm strikes. His nose, crookedly slanting rightward, leaked bloody mucus.

Running full steam, they reengaged their classmate's assaulter.

Piper slipped between Navi'el's legs, raking her fingers along the moon's ground to collect sediments and soot. Sliding a foot away, the residuum on her forehead calcified as she pieced them together.

Julien swung his sickles with the desire to execute a decapitation. Alas, Navi'el, quicker than a cheetah, let go of Noah, and grabbed hold of the descending blades. Overpowering the momentum, he squeezed.

One was snapped, the other was bent.

"Malleable and cheap," he said.

Downed to a knee, Julien stared incredulously at the remains of his metallic customizations. "No, my grace is supposed to be unbreakable. How could something like this happen?"

"Because the Celortus fooled you," vilified Navi'el, breaking the bent sickle. "The graces they've saturated Elehominum with are nothing but bastardized offshoots of the one, true grace: darkness."

"You're wrong; they wouldn't lie to us!"

Hearing Piper's detraction, Navi'el spun to meet her, but was stabbed in the navel with a prickled moon rock. The greenish-black mineral was attached to a pole of other thinner yet equally sharp rocks. He tried to backstep, but a half-conscious Noah hugged his legs. The rock harpoon dug deeper, squishy sounds certifying that its endless barbs were effortlessly slicing into unprotected meat.

Hands reverting to an unwelded state of gold, Julien gathered the sickle shards and jabbed them into Navi'el's lower back. Swarms of winged, black insects flew from his gashes, gnawing at the Elehominum's necks.

They were slapped like mosquitos, withering to slickened bits with a single swat.

While the Elehominum dealt with the swarm, Navi'el pulled the pole out of his navel. He knocked Piper six feet away with a successful swing, cut Noah's chin, and launched it at Sister Agnieszka's spine.

Diving in front of her, Julien pushed out his hands to block the incoming prickles and edges. The rocks disintegrated, sooty clouds stinging his eyes. Blinking and fanning his face, he saw his classmate's demise.

Navi'el stood over Noah, bathing him in orange stardust. His body underwent convulsions as color drained from his skin and clothes alike.

"Lord in Heaven, no," Sister Agnieszka yowled, witnessing the ordeal.

"Somebody…anybody…tell me what's goin' on," said an agonized Blair.

Noah had become a shadow, orange flares coiling his waist. Going limp, the purple wolf fell from a tree branch. Howling weakly, it vanished.

Ya-heemah scratched the eyes of the surviving wolves, sending them tumbling before the hostages. "Yes, non-believers, tell your friend what has transpired."

"Noah's gone," Julien promulgated, teeth clenched. "His Kindred Spirit, too."

Jonty stirred in his sleep.

"He was just a boy," bemoaned Sister Agnieszka.

"Don't let that go unanswered; you gotta torture him for what he's done to Noah," Blair bitterly outsourced, wriggling in a pool of sweat.

"You don't have to tell me twice. This is personal now," said Julien.

"Tell me what the tipping point was," Navi'el exacerbated. "Was it not when I strung you up on that noose, or when I kidnapped your derelict cousin?"

Piper limped, wiping blood from her bottom lip. "It was when you killed a Geordie."

"I've already forgotten his name," dismissed Navi'el.

"I'll make sure you always remember it," Piper guaranteed.

"Then attack me, colonizer," coaxed Navi'el,

wrenching the shards out of his back.

Tapping her forehead then the ground, Piper cultivated an acclivity of moon rocks. She climbed as quickly as her little legs would allow, ignoring scrapes and cuts that sullied her uniform.

Navi'el threw a shard at Julien, who had tried to blindside him, spearing his shoulder. With the stronger Elehominum down, he bustled to meet Piper at the top of the rock wall.

"Be still, Mr. Preux. I will come to you and nurse your injury," Sister Agnieszka said.

"No, you have to deliver our baby. I'll be fine," objected Julien, pulling at the shard.

A white-hot twinge shot through his shoulder, making him reevaluate his choice. Lying flat to alleviate the discomfort, he gained an upward view of the unfolding brawl.

The two climbers met atop the rock wall at the same time. Navi'el swung his shard at Piper's chest, but she ducked and struck his abdomen with her forearm. Winded, he doubled over in midair. Wrapping her arms around his neck to secure a front face-lock, she fell backward and drove his head through each layer of the wall. After splintering the last of the foundational rocks, he was motionless.

"You got him good, kiddo," Julien flattered. "Now put the finishing touch on him, and we can end this nightmare."

Hurdling, the Kindred Spirits locked their jaws onto Ya-heemah's ears and lugged it down the tree. They ripped them off and clawed its belly, spilling curdled goo. Swinging its tail to put distance between itself and those unforgiving wolves, the intergalactic jaguar turned and retreated. The heroic hounds gave chase, nipping at its hind legs.

"The youngest of our wards, dealing the deathblow to the Earth's biggest threat. I would move the sun and the stars if it meant Father Nigel could see this moment," said Sister Agnieszka.

Crawling, Piper grabbed the shard. She rolled Navi'el over and mounted him. His mouth curved into a smile and he hosed her with an orange blast. The projection's force was strong enough to elevate her petite, blackening body so high that even Blair could see the color drain from it.

"No," Julien cried.

Blair pounded the ground, electric discharges stiffening her hair. "We'll send ya to Hell for this one!"

Navi'el's birthmark halted its life-sapping ray. Piper dropped onto the rubble, a line of flares tethering her to Noah.

"My…daughter…was a fighter," driveled Ellis, finally joining the other hostages in sleep.

Eroding, the brown wolf winked out of sight. Capitalizing on the distraction of its sudden disappearance, Ya-heemah gashed the pack alpha's maw.

"I won't let you hurt any more of them," remonstrated Sister Agnieszka, pointing that MP5 at Navi'el.

Julien stood and stepped in front of the gun, staring coldly into Navi'el's eyes.

"Bullets aren't the answer. I know what I've gotta do," he shouted, removing the shard lodged in his shoulder.

CHAPTER XIII

and pressed to his gaping wound, Julien left a bloody trail as he initiated the apocalyptic confrontation with Navi'el. He ignored Sister Agnieszka's spirited Polish prayers and the warring animals' screeches. Feet dragging, his eyes were trained on the murderer of his classmates. He did not blink nor speak, manipulated by the spiteful rage within him. Reverberant booms loosened its mind control. Pausing, he peered over his incised shoulder. Glossed in sweat, Blair's bent knees radiated vermilion lightning bolts.

The electrical discharges extinguished stars, showering the moon in a bright orange-red hue.

"Push harder," Sister Agnieszka said, using her fingers to pull back Blair's cervical opening.

Blair squealed thunderously, expelling more bolts. One ricocheted off a star, electrocuting Ya-heemah's whiskers. Taking advantage of that unintentional assist, the lone wolf sliced its jaguar adversary's nose to ribbons. The electricity routed between their bodies, shocking both to the point of collapse.

Though ever so slightly, Ya-heemah was the first

to move.

"I won't let anybody or anything hurt my baby," manifested Julien, rings armoring his knuckles.

"I will not hurt your newborn, though it would be an eye for an eye. My people were far more humane than the heartless Europeans," Navi'el asseverated. "No harm will come to it from my hands, but it'll starve to death in the New World."

Julien's fingertips switched between the Seven Metals of Combat. "I never hated anyone until I met you. You took two of the only real friends I've ever had, nabbed my cousin like he was some runaway slave, and now you're making threats against my kid? I'm gonna take my time and enjoy killing you."

The incessant shifting stopped when a shinier coat of gold plated his hands, and black hoops ringed his knuckles. He perspired, veins bulging in his neck.

"I've braved Black Gold Mode before; you will taste no victories," Navi'el envisaged.

Julien throttled him, and delivered a volley of right-handed jabs.

Navi'el clapped Julien's ears, unsteadying his equilibrium. When the last standing Elehominum's legs crossed, he went for an over-the-shoulder arm drag.

Julien landed on his feet and connected with a spinning backfist.

"You've survived long enough," formalized Navi'el, ring imprints welting his cheek.

Birthmark twitching, he shot dual blasts of stardust.

Julien recast his hands to golden axes accented with black, burnished edges. He cut the projectiles in half, and they dwindled to an orange paste. Suddenly, his eyesight blurred and his heart's pace quickened. Assuming that Ya-heemah had stealthily poisoned him, he looked to where the bigendered being was last seen.

It had the golden wolf pinned down, biting into the gilded fur of its chest.

"Don't blame my god; Ya-heemah is not the reason you're sick," Navi'el said. "You have impressive skills. Pity they come at such a high price."

Tottering, Julien fell onto his bottom.

"Black Gold Mode does a Goldevoire more harm than good. It's weakening your immune system, and overstressing your muscles," diminished Navi'el, kicking Julien in the side of his head.

Downed, he saw Sister Agnieszka dodge lightning strikes as she repeatedly assured Blair the baby was almost out.

Navi'el stepped into Julien's line of vision. "Your great-grandfather would have seen that kick coming. He'd be ashamed if you were to get hit by this, too."

He shot another blast. Crossing his axe-hands over his chest, Julien deflected it and the pressure greatly propelled its summoner backward.

"You're a quick thinker, but sharp wits won't suffice in preserving your rundown school of magical misfits, much less the world," Navi'el undervalued, his slide concluding at Ya-heemah's backside.

Nearly botching a kip-up, Julien pursued him with fast but awkward, sloppy steps.

"The fighting spirit of a Haitian, lessened to a crash dummy who blindly guards his people's oppressors."

Navi'el threw a punch but Julien, in his wobbly

motions, avoided it. He wildly swung his all-metal enhancements, slashing a layer of skin off the High Chief's unprotected thigh.

"What makes you think you can disrespect my school's alumni, when Emily was bragging about incest, and one of your Commando buddies got caught trying to feel up a little girl?"

"That Commando was searching Henrietta to see if she had found any of the weapons your class left behind before we shipped you to Noyeur Atlantis," said Navi'el, struggling to put weight on his disfigured leg. "Your statement only proves me correct; Europeans are the true savages. Here's food for thought: Emily was more important than you know."

"Take your cryptic hints and stick 'em where the sun doesn't shine. I know all I need to know," Julien derogated, swinging for the same spot.

Performing a picture-perfect cartwheel without the use of his hands, Navi'el eluded a slash that was sure to amputate what remained of his leg.

Spinning with his arms outstretched, Julien missed his target, but managed to knock Ya-heemah off of the golden wolf. Growling, it righted itself and set him in its sights. Rolling onto all fours, the golden wolf squared up to Navi'el.

They had changed dance partners.

"You shall perish in my arms," Ya-heemah said, making a grab for Julien.

Side-stepping, he axed a paw. The impact of the chop floored his alien adversary. Inspired by its roaring shrieks, he hacked away until the paw was fully severed. He was about to repeat the barbaric process on the other paw when he heard the trilling of drills.

The golden wolf was trying to impale Navi'el, but he continuously flipped out of its range. With each landing, he kicked the wolf's testicles.

Julien's momentary lapse in attention gave Ya-heemah time to regrow its paw, and trip his legs from under him. The gloomy halos vented from its spots amassed, binding his waist and knees.

"Mortals are so easily distracted," it besmirched, mounting him. "Your story ends here. So begins the New World's creation saga."

Ya-heemah's mouth widened as it sucked in stars, and breathed a slowly extending beam of heat.

Julien feverishly turned his head from the curdling beam's crimson tip, certain his face would decompose if touched. He focused on Sister Agnieszka and Blair, refusing to show fear. A shrilling blare sounded, followed by a scream. Turning toward the direction from which the turmoil came, he saw Navi'el's body, gored and limp, fly through the air. The golden wolf sped to Julien's defense, successfully tackling and boring into the arcane jaguar's right eye. Its hollers of misery shook the moon.

"You shall pay dearly for your insolence, you impudent dog!" Ya-heemah declaimed.

The golden wolf's drill penetrated the back of its skull.

Cutting the binds, Julien jumped in celebration. "Can't destroy the Earth if you've been blinded in both eyes. Wait until my Kindred Spirit takes the other one!"

An alabaster arrow punctured his left calf, toppling him.

Laid on his stomach, Navi'el held a waxen bow.

"I told you that you wouldn't win, but you thought differently. Now look at you, alone and crippled," he moralized, panting.

Julien uselessly cleaved at the arrow as a warm stiffness immobilized his leg. "If I'd have known you were hiding a bow and arrow, I would've been on the lookout. Guess I shouldn't have believed you wanted a fair fight. All that crap you talked about your tribe having honor was bull."

"Nothing was hidden," Navi'el said, his bow dissolving. "I forged the weapon seconds ago in my mind, and what you see is its physical manifestation. Had you been mentally strong enough to only think of the hate you have for me, you might've stood a sliver of a chance, but since you aren't, Black Gold Mode has failed you."

"Should've known an underhanded phony like you would find a loophole. You ought to use some Indian warpaint to write 'cheater' on your forehead," animadverted Julien.

"And you ought to accept your fate," Navi'el finalized, propping himself up on his forearms.

Blood flowed from his drilled abdominals as he fired a rocket of stardust.

Julien was hit square on his chin. Neck whiplashing, he slumped in a swampy pool of the colors that once pigmented his hair, skin, and jumpsuit.

"Let this be a lesson to you: you are no Jean-Renee," reprehended Navi'el, dragging himself closer.

Julien shivered as his hands defaulted to their normal conditions. "What's…happening…to me?"

"Same thing that happened to your friends,"

Navi'el accounted, arriving at his side. "Ya-heemah taught me, long ago, the deadly effects of aged stardust on Elehominum. Your brain is entering a vegetative state, and your organs are beginning to fail. It's a wonder you can still talk at this moment."

Julien tried to speak, but his lips would not fully part. All he could do was make raspy, short-winded croaks.

"Before you take your last breath, you should know that you and your friends made history," alluded Navi'el, plowing a hand into the moon's surface. "No Elehominum has ever died on the Omnipotent Continent before tonight. I had you solve my riddle and follow me, just to bring you back to where you've already been. You weren't a wise wolf; you were merely a dog chasing its tail."

He unearthed the gatekeeper's ribcage, silver embers flickering within it.

Julien shed a gold tear that simmered the color pool.

"It was Ya-heemah's will for you to die on a land that shifts itself, so you could see how quickly your existence will be forgotten. Goodbye, Wolven one," Navi'el sentenced.

Streaking, flare lines roped Julien's wrists and ankles, and tethered him to Noah and Piper. His limbs grew increasingly numb, and he wet himself.

Julien lost all sensation as the golden wolf's drills warbled decrepitly. Fading, it left Ya-heemah eyeless but alive.

Defeated, Julien was forced to witness the outcome of his failure. Vermilion lightning bolts annihilated ten stars, their explosions providing a drizzle of that noxious dust. Countless monoliths rose from the moon's craters, teal glyphs inscribed on each rockface. Black globes hoisted them, the one nearest Julien modeled after present-day Earth.

Hand pressed to his chest wound, Navi'el approached Sister Agnieszka and Blair. His footsteps were lumbering and inelegant.

"I've waited for this moment for a lifetime. I'd wait a million more if it meant reclaiming the land our Great Jaguar Entity intended for my tribe. The extinction of your people is the price that must be paid for their thievery, and for attacking a god."

Purring feebly, Ya-heemah clumsily sniffed around for its displaced eyes.

"I will lay down my life before I let you hurt this child, or its mother," Sister Agnieszka said, turning with her gun aimed.

Navi'el uppercutted her, and she went flying into a monolith.

"The rest of England is now under a peaceful sleep spell. I would have done the same for you, if you weren't so burdensome," he foisted, exhaustedly falling to a knee. "Enjoy your nap, Agnieszka. It's the last you'll ever take."

"Kill the girl and the child," orchestrated Ya-heemah.

"In this moment, watch the moon eclipse the sun as the newborn's blood begins to run," Navi'el recited.

The High Chief gathered his reserve ounce of strength. He reached for Blair's legs but they spread, and a charge of argent light hollowed his torso. The light broadened and blasted him against the sequoia that held the hostages.

Quaking, the monoliths crumbled.

"No, I did not foresee this. This cannot be true," expostulated Ya-heemah, a rounded slab of stone crushing its spine.

Blair sat up, cradling a placenta-soaked baby in her arms.

"Gu'laar toka ruja. Peace to my slain brothers and sisters, and to the god we served unconditionally. I was so close to avenging you," Navi'el grieved, his body pruning. "Someday, someone will succeed."

"Say that when you see 'em in Hell," said Blair.

Glowing, the baby's pink fingers discharged a surge of light that vaporized Navi'el. It then went through the tree bark, and changed its trajectory to Ya-heemah. Aflame and wailing, the spatial jaguar withered to a charcoaled skeleton.

Face covered in blood mixed with dust, Sister Agnieszka crawled from under the rock wreckage. A pebble was stuck in her right nostril.

"Unto us a savior is born, the one whose soul bears immortal light."

"Just wish everyone lived to see us win," Blair repined, woefully surveying the color-sapped bodies of her fallen classmates.

Wiping away a tear, Sister Agnieszka gritted her teeth.

"They'll be legends, Ms. Bisping. Your child will proudly represent the legacy of those who paved the way for her and…"

Sister Agnieszka's declaration was interrupted by

the sequoia's branches dropping its apples. The baby giggled as the tree bark shed. Eight small figures cut through the cambium cell layer, each composed of a different grace. Circling their heads were halos that dispensed infrared gases.

"We cannot thank you enough for the sacrifices you have made," said one Celorti.

"It is because of you that the Earth is free of Navi'el's tyranny," another said.

Blair looked to Julien. "All the gratitude in the world ain't gonna bring him, or our friends, back from the dead."

"Your wishes do not go unheard," the Celortus collectively lilted.

Their gases became color-washed, reflecting each individualized grace. Converging, they engulfed Julien, Noah, and Piper.

"What're they doin' to 'em?" asked Blair.

"I dare not hazard a guess, Ms. Bisping," Sister Agnieszka waived. "But, if I were a betting woman, I would say our hearts are about to be cleared of troubles."

The orange tethers that came after Navi'el's stardust blasts dulled and wilted, worming themselves back beneath the moon's surface. Color steadily returned to the Wolven scholars who were thought to be casualties.

"Graced children, arise in the name of Edenshire Academy," compelled the Celortus, their halos enlarging.

Julien fluttered with new life, his breathing rapid. Yawning, Noah and Piper stretched their limbs but tensed upon overstimulation.

"They're alive, they're alive," Blair reveled.

"Praise the Lord! My wards have triumphed over evil," venerated Sister Agnieszka.

"We saved the Earth, for real this time," Julien philosophized, carefully righting himself. "And there's our baby. Is it a boy or a girl?"

"A bad gyal, just like her mumma," bragged Blair. "Turned Navi'el and that jaguar into crumbs. Wouldn't expect nothin' less from my kid, especially since she's got that immortal light."

"She is the messiah the books spoke of," Sister Agnieszka said.

The red lightning formed a heart that washed over Blair, cleansing the baby of amniotic fluid.

"Waged war with the biggest, scariest monsters, went to faraway places, and now we finally get to see her coming. Imagine that," cogitated Noah, rubbing his nose.

"We won," Piper summed.

Smiles were on the faces of every combat veteran.

The smile on Julien's face, however, waned when he noticed the sequoia's deterioration. "What about my cousin, and everyone else that Navi'el kidnapped?"

"They, along with the rest of the country, should be awaking from his sleeping spell within the hour. We do not sense any critical conditions, but it would be wise to go home at once," said the Celortus. "Our essences allow Elehominum and their envoys to breathe and move safely on the Omnipotent Continent. The sorcery Navi'el used to bring the hostages here shall unquestionably wear off soon."

"I do not mean to sound ungrateful, but my wards are in no state to be carrying fully grown adults,"

Sister Agnieszka diverged.

Pointing their index fingers at the hostages, the Celortus removed every one of their head coverings and suspended them in midair.

"Fear not, truehearted envoy," appeased the Celortus, lowering the debilitated four into the lengthening portal. "We shall transport them with care."

Julien limped to the baby, and kissed both of her hands. "Well, we cheated death and the world's safe, but my parents are still gonna kill me when they find out I'm a dad. How the heck am I supposed to convince them to let me come to England more than once a year?"

"Dunno but she deserves to have a full-time father, so ya better start thinkin' about how you're gonna do it," Blair strong-armed.

"We shall cast a false memory charm that will make them think they've already known of the pregnancy, and have agreed to the terms set forth by the child's mother," conspired the Celortus. "A separate charm will be used for every other afflicted person. They'll assume it was all a bad dream."

"This *does* feel like some trippy dream, but I don't want to ever wake up. For the first time in my life, I'm a hero," Julien said.

"A superhero," reworded Noah.

"You are what you believe yourselves to be. Go forth and enjoy the world you've purified," ratified the Celortus. "Your envoy will prepare your commencement ceremony."

"My wards have earned this honor," Sister Agnieszka committed.

The Elehominum excitedly speculated about the event's purpose as the nun herded them through the portal.

———————⊷⟡⊶———————

Julien, Noah, and Piper were given strict orders to go to their dorm rooms and sleep, assured that the Celortus would return the hostages to their homes. Sister Agnieszka took Blair and the baby to Edenshire Academy's clinic for post-birth treatment.

"I'd suggest a biblical name, Ms. Bisping. They're timeless."

"How? I've never met a Ruth, Esther, or Judith in my life. I'm thinkin' maybe something French."

Ear pressed to his door, Julien listened to their conversation about potential names until they were too far to hear. He then reclined on his bed, drowsily re-reading the letter he intended for his parents. Yawning thrice, sleep overcame him. He dreamed of walking an endless road with Jean-Renee.

Sunlight shined through his window, waking him with the help of Sister Agnieszka's Dutch handbell.

"Dawn's broke already," Julien said, rolling out of bed. "Hope that ringing means breakfast is ready. I could eat a whole horse."

Leaving his room, he saw Piper sleepily descending the stairs. Straggling behind her was Noah, pressing an ice pack to his nose. He joined them in the walk to the bottom of the staircase. Their eyes enlarged at what they saw.

A sea of balloons covered the great hall's floor. Color-coded banners listing their names hung from the chandeliers. Cakes and pastries sat on one table, while baked beans, sausages, and raisin bread were on another. Blair breastfed at a separate table that held fruit baskets. The baby glowed with every suckle, the yellow cloth she was wrapped in expelling sparkles.

Near the school's entrance was Ellis, fitting glass doors onto a trophy case that held the Elehominum's confiscated weapons.

Sister Agnieszka rounded the staircase, holding four zaternium medals engraved with wolf pawprints. "Today is a good morning, scholars; the Celortus recovered everything Navi'el stole from the schoolgrounds. It is also the day you will formally be honored for your services to Edenshire, and be given your official class roles. Please align yourselves from youngest to oldest."

Her forehead was wrapped in bandages, prompting Julien to ask about her health. His question went unanswered as she moved to the front of their line.

"Ms. Woolgar, your craftiness has landed you the role of Architect," Sister Agnieszka said, adorning Piper with a medal. "You are in charge of making a crest that will represent your class. Also, any physical additions to the school, be they extra rooms or minor alterations to existing ones, must be approved by you."

Applauding her daughter's election, Ellis blew a toy kazoo.

"Mam, you're embarrassing me," tee-heed Piper, her cheeks red.

Sister Agnieszka stepped to Noah next and gave him his medal.

"Though painfully stubborn and disobedient at times, you're an avid researcher, half-cut with knowledge. Mr. Satterly, you are now the Keeper of Records. It is your job to create and maintain files relevant to your classmates and myself, which will be stored in the Restricted Area of the Library of Solstice."

Noah smiled smugly. "Can we change the role title to 'Lore Master?' It sounds cooler, honestly."

Sister Agnieszka ignored him.

"Motherhood changes women, but I believe your intensity is eternal," she stated, placing a medal around Blair's neck. "As the Sergeant at Arms, you will make sure that your classmates are respectful during group discussions, no matter the topic. Those that are not will be subject to a penalty system that you alone have authority over."

"I'm the one that keeps everybody else in check? Bet," extracted Blair.

Sister Agnieszka loomed over Julien, faint snarls coming from the final medal.

"Father Nigel said you would be the Valedictorian of this class; he was correct. Citizens of foreign lands, whether Atlantean or otherwise, must appeal directly to you if they want to establish friendly relations. Laws governing Edenshire Academy will require your signature before they can go into effect. The Celortus will question you directly about anything that seems amiss, including marks and the general state of the building. I will advise you to the fullest extent of my abilities, but you now have the final say in decisions related to how our school is run. You have your unrivaled intelligence, bravery, and natural leadership to thank for this role, Mr. Preux."

"I couldn't have done it without you all. Regardless

of how tough this role will be, I'm going to do what's best for the school," Julien contracted. "But I am curious about something: can I make my first pronouncement right now?"

The Elehominum whispered amongst themselves.

Suspicious, Sister Agnieszka hesitantly awarded him the medal. "And what would that be, Mr. Preux?"

"Ava getting kidnapped after two of her wards were killed is what caused the school's mandate for two envoys, if I'm not mistaken," recalled Julien. "No disrespect to her, but I think you've proven that you're more than capable of doing what she couldn't. I'm rolling back that mandate; you are *the* Headmistress of Edenshire Academy."

"Mr. Preux, I would be uncomfortable accepting such responsibilities unless I had the full support of the entire…"

"We already told ya how we feel. Nothin' has changed," Blair cut Sister Agnieszka off.

"You're all we need in this life of sin," accredited Noah.

"Nobody's as good as you," Piper hyped.

"To the new Headmistress and the scholars who saved the world. Long live Edenshire Academy," said Ellis, pouring herself a glass of brandy and toasting.

The Elehominum raised their fists in solidarity and bellowed, "Long live Edenshire Academy!"

EPILOGUE

In preparation for her increased workload, Sister Agnieszka received further combat training from the Celortus on the Omnipotent Continent. She created new courses for Edenshire Academy's curriculum, including Intro to Old Celortian and non-Euclidean geometry. The school doubled as a year-round house, free of room and board, under her guardianship. She secretly taught Julien and Blair about an envoy's responsibilities, and asked them to promise to succeed her whenever she was no longer fit to hold the role.

Julien returned to Washington D.C. in August of 2017. Thanks to the Celortus' false memory charm, he was able to convince his parents that they had allowed him to go to a boarding school in Newcastle to be closer to his daughter. After claiming to have lost his teeth in a rough game of soccer, he flew back to Newcastle and began his term as Valedictorian. Sister Agnieszka called in a few favors and got him accepted into the Gosforth Institute, a private all-boys school. He went on to graduate from Northumbria University with a Bachelor of Science in Biochemistry. He made plans to marry Blair that summer, all the while establishing an immigration system for persons impacted by Navi'el's savagery. The first wave were displaced Atlanteans.

Blair finished her time in secondary school with the best marks of her educational career. She then went immediately into the workforce, becoming a correctional officer at a juvenile prison. Using the prison's resources, she found an affordable drug addiction treatment clinic and checked her mother into it. Despite the hectic environment and long hours of her profession, Blair honored her duties as the Sergeant at Arms. The only classmate she had to paddle regularly was Noah, because he often talked out of turn or made inappropriate jokes. She married Julien on a particularly hot July day, proudly taking his last name in front of her sober mother and his parents, who, for some reason, felt like they hadn't met her prior to the wedding.

Noah elected to withdraw from traditional schooling, opting to be educated solely at Edenshire Academy. Sister Agnieszka tutored him in grammar, maths, and sciences, but stressed how important "learning at the source" was for true scholars. Every six months, she gave him money to visit a foreign country to discover new cultures. Although enamored with the food and weather of Trinidad and Tobago, Noah settled in Atlantis after meeting Umar's sister, Uria. They married shortly after their first conversation and had a total of three children. Noah was later appointed diplomat by Emperor Cain, further strengthening the ties between Earth and Atlantis. Despite living in Atlantis, he has remained diligent in upkeeping all files that tell the account of Navi'el and Ya-heemah's defeat.

Piper's design for a class crest was a quartz sculpture of a wolf pup with four tails. She remained loyal to her religious roots, attending exclusively Catholic schools and observing holidays. After going with Ellis on a missionary trip to Kenya, she decided to study at the University of Nairobi. There, Piper gained degrees in Geography and Archaeology. Her writings on Mesopotamian civilizations are critically acclaimed, and she is rumored to be in talks with the History channel for a five-part documentary on the gods of Sumer. Piper's biggest contribution to Edenshire Academy is the Woolgar Gallery, a collective display of items significant to the school's lineage.

As for the child whose soul bears immortal light, her name is *Madeline*.

A final discourse with Nevelious Jordan

Nevelious Jordan has completed his Wolven Scholar trilogy. Mr. Jordan's contractual obligations with Shatteringham Books have now been met with the release of *Jungle of Eclipses*, the third installment of the series. Today, Shatteringham Books' newest intern, Ashton Price, picks his brain to answer the lingering questions we had regarding his creative process.

This is your third time writing a book. What does that mean to you?
It means a lot of things, really, but more than anything else, it means that I did my characters justice. This is the culmination of all those long nights of writing and editing.

Walk me through the process of wrapping up a story.
First, I re-read *School of the Wolven Way* and *Pedigree Penitentiary* to get back into the headspace of my fictional worlds. Then, I plotted out every single thing that I wanted to happen. I did those things because I wanted to have certain callbacks to the previous two books, so my readers could say stuff like, "Oh, I remember that!" The pre-writing phase was a little longer for this book because I wanted to take my time with the story's ending.

You mentioned callbacks; what was your favorite one to include and why?

That's easy: Abigail and Amelia. I referenced their deaths in *School of the Wolven Way*, and I wasn't entirely sure if they'd make it into the actual, on-going story in a major way. Then, I got the idea of having Noah and Piper, their old classmates, fight resurrected versions of them. It was a nice way of showing off other graces (hail and snow) without them being attached to heroes, and it gave Noah and Piper a moment to really shine. Their fight scenes were the most fun to write because of the emotional connection between the four of them.

Klara was a callback. Was she originally intended to make an appearance in the book?

She totally was. I needed a way to explain more of the Mavkardia's origins and she was it. When I first mentioned her in *School of the Wolven Way*, I knew she would appear in the final book and be a potential factor in the Elehominum's fight with Navi'el.

What, if anything, do you think differentiates Navi'el from other literary villains?

He isn't senselessly killing. Everything he does is because he wants to restore his people, who were destroyed by events beyond his control. Navi'el was, in some twisted sense, a beacon of hope for them. Aside from that, I don't know of any literary villains that came from the moon. Him having that sort of background gave me ideas for his looks, attacks, and the general concept of Ya-heemah.

Is this where the story ends for the graced children?
I do have more ideas floating around in my head for Edenshire Academy, but it all depends on how the series as a whole is received. For now, this is the end.

It's been a pleasure speaking with you, Mr. Jordan. Please say we'll get one last poem.
I wouldn't have it any other way.

True to Our Elements

Divinely chosen to walk this path
I study at the most secretive institution
Learning of my elemental abilities and sacred
math
Bred to be Earth's sole solution

Metal, electricity, terra firma, ectoplasm
Lava, hail, verdure, water, snow
As we master these graces, our muscles spasm
And our insight into the cosmos begins to grow

Wolven by any other name
Heavenly animalistic
Organized, hungry, and impossible to tame
A pack mentality that is ritualistic

Bonded in blood and war
We are the selected few
Who serve and protect forevermore
To these elements, we remain true

www.ingramcontent.com/pod-product-compliance
Lightning Source LLC
Chambersburg PA
CBHW050344030726
47503CB00008B/2609